THE QUEEN AGAINST DEFOE

And Other Stories

Also by Stefan Heym

THE KING DAVID REPORT

The Queen Against Defoe

And Other Stories

BY STEFAN HEYM

HODDER AND STOUGHTON
LONDON SYDNEY AUCKLAND TORONTO

This collection first printed in Great Britain 1975. ISBN 0 340 19556 8
Reproduced from the original setting by arrangement with Lawrence Hill & Company.

 Printed in Great Britain for Hodder & Stoughton Limited, St Paul's House, Warwick Lane, London EC4P 4AH by Cox & Wyman Ltd., London, Fakenham and Reading

Contents

THE QUEEN AGAINST DEFOE 9
From the Notes of one Josiah Creech

A VERY GOOD SECOND MAN 61

ACROSS THE FENCE 77

THE WACHSMUTH SYNDROME 95

THE CREATOR & THE COMMISSARS 115
by J. ROBERT MOSKIN
An Encounter with Stefan Heym

The Queen Against Defoe

From the Notes of one Josiah Creech

The following was lent to me in 1944, in London, by Miss Agnes Creech, after a night partly spent conversing on affairs both current and historical. The papers, Miss Creech said, had been in her family for several hundred years. When I came back the next evening to return the manuscript and to present her with a bottle of gin and two cartons of American cigarettes, in which she had expressed an interest, the house in which Miss Creech plied her trade was gone and so was she.

I have done little editing on the notes her ancestor jotted down, except to modernise the spelling and to replace the abbreviations of the time by the full word.

S.H.

The Queen Against Defoe
From the Notes of one Josiah Creech

December 18, 1702

. . . it being a raw day. Despite his furs and the fire burning away, my Lord sat shivering as he perused the pages of a booklet. Having finished, he meticulously reattached to its pages the assorted correspondence by which it had come to his desk, passed the matter to me, and inquired, "I take it, Mr. Creech, that you are not unfamiliar with this anonymous work, lately come out, and entitled *The Shortest Way with the Dissenters*. Pray, what is your opinion?"

I stepped to the light and noted the contents of the topmost letter attached. It was addressed to my Lord, the Earl of Nottingham, in his capacity as Secretary of State, Southern Department, and signed by Lord Godolphin, the Lord Treasurer, who acquainted my Lord with the sense of several members of the Government that my Lord should endeavour to discover the author of the libel.

"Well, Mr. Creech," says my Lord in the nasal tone usual to him when impatient, "has your tongue clove to your palate?"

"The pamphlet, your Lordship," says I, "has created much excitement in the coffee houses and some turmoil on the streets, particularly in view of the bill pending in the Commons against the Dissenters. But people are of various minds on this work, and indeed it seems a thing of many colours."

"The truth, Mr. Creech," says he, chewing on his thin lower lip, "is either black or white."

"I have talked to men prominent in the High Church," says I, "who have praised this booklet to the skies, and who prize it above any literary work except the Holy Bible and the Sacred Comments, and it has wrought terror among the dissenting tribe, who fear for their trade, their posts, their money and even their lives. In essence, as your Lordship will have noted, it says little more than the good Dr. Sacheverell has said in his recent sermons, inspired by her Majesty's opening speech from the throne, mainly in his sermon at Oxford about raising the bloody banner of defiance against the heretics, except our author says it more prettily, and with better logic to it and with greater acumen."

"So you deem it a laudable piece, on the whole, Mr. Creech?" says he.

Unfortunately Lord Godolphin had failed to specify in his letter whether he and his powerful friends wished my Lord to discover the author of the libel for the purpose of rewarding or of punishing him. "On the other hand," says I, "there are equally stout supporters of the Established Church who maintain that you may think of disposing of your Dissenters in the manner suggested, but that it's an ill service to the good cause to proclaim this from the rooftops, as does the unknown author."

At this, my Lord regarded me at his most dismal, inquiring, "And which view do you lean to, Mr. Creech?"

"'Tis an awkward thing," says I, "to judge a matter without your superior's prior opinion."

My Lord Nottingham toyed with his exceedingly long fingers but remained silent.

"It cannot be denied," says I, culling from the libel in my hand, "that much of what is printed herein seems true. 'Tis well known that *the Dissenters, though dealt with most leniently by the Church* and at worst *shipped to New England to enjoy the privilege of erecting a new colony, rewarded that kindness by butchering one King and deposing another*. And isn't the author justified in asking how they did treat the Clergy *in the time of their glorious Commonwealth, sharing the Church lands among their soldiers and turning her Ministers out to starve?*"

My Lord pulled his furs about him and continued his gloom.

"And doesn't the author speak equally true," says I, taking a few lines from this page and some from that, "when he declares that *now that the Gentlemen of England are protected and encouraged by a Church of England Queen, the time has come to free the nation from the viperous brood that have so long sucked the blood of their Mother, and to pull up this heretical Weed of Sedition that has so long disturbed the Peace of the Church and poisoned the good corn?*"

My Lord moved closer to the fire and stared into it darkly.

"And isn't it obvious," says I, quoting further, "that *to show mercy to the Dissenters now will be more barbarous to our own children and to posterity, when our Church would be swallowed up in Schism, Faction, Enthusiasm and Confusion*? And hasn't your Lordship himself called it *a shame to a Christian Government*, quite as does this author, that *an offence against God and the Church and the dignity of Religion may be bought off for a fine of five shillings*, when men are *hung for far lesser sins and banished for trifles?*"

At which my Lord Nottingham coughed and spat into the fire.

Since no other comment was forthcoming, I thought it wisest to let the booklet's author speak. "*If one severe law were made*, says he," says I, "*and punctually executed, that whoever was found in a Conventicle should be banished from the nation, and the Preacher be hanged, we should soon see an end to the tale. For this end,* says he *has, Providence given such a Parliament! such a Gentry! and such a Queen! as we never had before. What with Popery on one hand*, says he, *and Schismatics on the other, the Church of England has been crucified between two thieves. Now, let us crucify the thieves!*"

"Crucify . . ." says my Lord, thoughtfully. "Sounds good, Mr. Creech, doesn't it?"

The flames threw shadows on my Lord's countenance, shrouding its expression. But something in his tone cautioned me.

"A bit too good, perhaps," says I.

"Quite," says he. . . .

December 27, 1702

. . . God installed no printing presses in the Garden of Eden, my Lord Nottingham once told me, consequently the devil must have invented the alphabet. I am inclined to believe 'tis true. How else to explain the deplorable circumstance that everything un-Christian and subversive is written so much more cleverly and effectively than the upright God-fearing tracts of the Established Church?

To wit, *The Shortest Way with the Dissenters*. There's small doubt, now, that the Right-thinking Clergy and Gentry have been had for a fool, although many refuse to admit it and continue to say that *The Shortest Way* is the only proper way. For which several were dragged off and beaten by the mob before Christmas. Now, in Cornhill and Cheapside, in shops and taverns and coffee-houses, people say that this libel is a satire, writ by a sharp pen and with tongue in cheek, to show up the High Church and Tory party; and there are those that whisper that it's a plot by the followers of the late King William against the present Government and against my Lord Nottingham especially, and I have rarely seen my Lord in such high dudgeon as when he told me to *get that man* because he was a greater danger to State and Church than the armies of France.

So I invited Mr. Robert Stephens, Queen's Messenger in charge of matters of the press; but he sent word that he was suffering from the gout, and so I saw him at his quarters, in the midst of a confusion of dirty bedding, and unwashed beer mugs and stale foods, him cursing the day he was born and looking, under his stocking cap, more than ever like *Robin Hog*, which is the name given him by the literati.

"Mr. Stephens," says I, "now who is the author of this, *The Shortest Way* et cetera?"

The small eyes between the swollen lids turned ceilingwards. "I wish I knew, Mr. Creech," says he. "'Twould be a service to the Christian cause and to some great men in Government to put the author in Newgate; but his name is Anonymous from the County of Nowhere, and have the goodness, Mr. Creech, to look at my foot, the size of an elephant's, how am I to catch so nimble a ghost in my present condition?"

"You don't think with your foot," says I.

At this, Mr. Hog frowned fiercely and then pointed his stubby finger towards a paper lying on his table between the remains of a pheasant and a packet of snuff. "'Tis the list of my clientele," says he, groaning, and asks, "did you ever have a toothache in your foot, Mr. Creech?"

So we began to winnow his roster, eliminating this name for the man's character, that one for his style, a third for other good reasons. In the end, few names remained, the most likely among them that of Mr. Daniel Ffooe, or Fooe, or Foe, or DeFoe: formerly a hosier in Freeman's yard, then gone bankrupt, and now owner of a brick and pantile works near Tilbury-Fort in Essex; author of a number of pamphlets and pasquils, but mainly of the *True-Born Englishman*, a long poem in defence of Dutch King William, in which it is claimed that there is no such animal as a True-Born Englishman, but that we're all a race of bastards.

"Unfortunately, Mr. Stephens," says I, since the days of the Star Chamber are gone, we'll have to have some proof, even if we must manufacture it."

"Pray give me the libel, Mr. Creech," says Mr. Hog, "and hold up that candle."

With this, he tested the paper between his finger tips, fondling it as though it were a wench's tit, and peered at the print, turning the pages against the light, and comparing letters and lines, muttering to himself all the while and puffing his mouth and smacking his lips in utter intentness.

"Mr. Creech," says he, finally, "try the printshop of George Croome; but see that you take along one or two constables, for the prentices and journeymen printers are notorious ruffians and unconscionable. And pass me that pitcher from over there; 'tis some beer left in it, I think. . . ."

January 2, 1703

. . . found, at Croome's printshop, several hundred sheets, unbound, of *The Shortest Way*, and the type standing and ready for another printing. Mr. Croome protesting that we broke into and searched his premises without due warrant, I calmed him by explaining that we well understood his printing this pamphlet in the belief that he was benefiting the Clergy and all honest men, and he could spare himself great trouble and prosecution if he told us the name of the author. Happy at so easy an escape, the printer admitted his belief that the author was Mr. Edward Bellamy of Southwark, who had delivered the manuscript to him together with a sum more than half covering the expense of the first edition and had paid in full after delivery, that Mr. Edward Bellamy had had the first edition carted off and then returned to request a second, larger printing, and now, a third.

I left the sheets in the care of the constables and returned post haste to Whitehall to report to my Lord on certain similarities between the libel that interested us and a second one entitled *The True-Born Englishman.* Also I requested a warrant for said Edward Bellamy who, I thought, was an old acquaintance having served some years ago as an informer, later become an agent for the Whig party, collecting intelligence and placing evidence and swearing false testimony, and in recent times doing odd services for anybody.

His Lordship was pleased to have an immediate warrant drawn up for Edward Bellamy and another, for good measure, for George Croome, the printer. "Mr. Creech," says he, "a bird in the hand is better than two on the roof, and with a stone doublet fitting close to his shoulders, this bird may sing more, and different, tunes."

"Your Lordship," says I, "we'll have them all singing shortly, and Mr. DeFoe will trill the prettiest."

So we apprehended Mr. Bellamy that same night and lodged him safely, and then I came in to him and found him seated on some straw and his wrists cuffed, and I inquired, "You do remember me, Mr. Bellamy?"

"Who wouldn't?" says he. "You're Mr. Josiah Creech."

Seeing that his hands shook and that he was half frightened out of his wits, I proceeded directly. "On that manuscript entitled *The Shortest Way with the Dissenters*, Mr. Bellamy," says I, "and which you transmitted to Mr. Croome, who was it that gave it to you?"

"I am not at liberty to tell," says he. "The gentleman made me pledge upon my honour, and I wouldn't break my word if my life depended on it."

"But your life depends on it, Mr. Bellamy," says I.

"How's that?" says he.

"I won't hold you in Newgate," says I. "I will let you go, but not before I have told the friends of a few men hung these last years by whose evidence they were made to swing."

"In that case, Mr. Creech," says he, "I don't mind telling you that the manuscript was given me by one Daniel Ffooe."

"You will swear to that?" says I.

"Upon my life," says he.

"Describe him," says I.

"He is a middle-sized, spare man," says he, "about forty years old, of sallow complexion, and dark brown hair, but wears a wig, a hooked nose, a sharp chin, grey eyes, and a large mole near his mouth."

"You are a good observer of men, Mr. Bellamy," says I.

"Observing men is part of my business, Mr. Creech," says he. "As it is of yours. . . ."

January 3, 1703

. . . dispatch now being of the essence, my Lord Nottingham that same night caused a warrant to be issued to Mr. Henry Allen, one of her Majesty's messengers in ordinary (Mr. Hog being excused due to his gout and exceeding obesity), requiring Mr. Allen to take to his assistance *a constable forthwith and make strict and diligent search for Daniel Foe, apprehend and seize him, together with his papers, for high crimes and misdemeanours,* and bring him before my Lord *to be examined and further dealt with according to law.* Further, *all mayors, justices of the peace, constables, and all other of her Majesty's officers civil and military, and loving subjects,* were ordered to assist Mr. Allen, *for which the paper in Mr. Allen's hand was to be to them and him sufficient warrant.* Having signed this in his own hand, my Lord then turned to me. "You will want to be of the party, Mr. Creech," says he, "and see that all goes smoothly. This Daniel Ffooe, at seeing himself discovered, might show himself a desperate and dangerous fellow."

"This Mr. DeFoe," says I, "will hardly be much different from other writers: quick with the pen but slow on the draw, lions on paper but poltroons on the street. I know a satchelful of them; your Lordship can meet them at any public feast where food is free and drink plentiful, smacking and guzzling, and looking about for anyone willing to throw a purse to them for their talents."

"I do not doubt your observations, Mr. Creech," says my Lord, "but we have entered upon an age in which your literary buffoons are becoming a proper scourge, and a statesman can be toppled by a sharp pen as easily as by gunpowder, and I wish to have a talk with Mr. Ffooe, before he can vanish in Whitefriars or another place of sanctuary."

So Mr. Allen and the constable and I mounted fast horses and arrived near Tilbury-Fort while it was still dark, hoping that word had not got to our man of the visit to Mr. Croome's printshop or of Mr. Bellamy having been taken. Some wretches early on their way to the brick kilns to work for Mr. DeFoe showed us to his house, easily the most substantial in the place, with a second storey and a fine roof. After tying the horses, the constable was stationed at the rear of the house and Mr. Allen knocked at the entrance gate, calling, to open up, on her Majesty's service.

There was much scurrying and lights went up, and a woman in a robe thrown over her nightdress opened, saying she was Mrs. DeFoe and her husband was gone to London the previous evening, and she did not know when his return might be expected. But Mr. Allen was not put off, and brushed by her into the house and past a brood of wailing children, five or six of them at the least, and up the stairs, tearing open each door as he came to it and finally exclaiming, "In London, ah, are you in London, then, sir, and have I the honour of speaking with Mr. Daniel Ffooe's ghost, sir?" To which I heard a calm voice replying that, yes, he had been on his way to the city, but after a few miles had turned back because a matter which required his presence at his factory had occurred to him, and finding his wife and family asleep on his return he had gone quietly to bed.

I then joined Mr. Allen on the upper storey and there, in the light of a candle, saw the partially dressed author of *The True-Born Englishman* and, presumably, *The Shortest Way with the Dissenters*, and found him looking much as Mr. Bellamy had described him, except that his complexion had paled to grey due to his having been shown the warrant and realising whither his journey was bound.

Mr. DeFoe inquired what misdemeanours and high crimes he was alleged to have committed that his Lordship the Earl of Nottingham in his own person wished to question him so hurriedly; but before I could reply that he would be enlightened in good time and directly by my Lord, Mr. Allen blundered, "that you are the author of a vicious and dangerous libel offensive to the Government and to her Majesty, sir, which might well land you in the pillory if not the gibbet, sir, the sooner the better, because persons like you, sir, are a disturbance to the peace and a disgrace to England."

"I deny all this," says Mr. DeFoe.

"Will you come along peaceably, sir," says Mr. Allen, "or do I use force."

"I will come along peaceably," says Mr. DeFoe, "but I'm a gentleman and should be attired decently to face his Lordship, and also must take along some apparel and money if I am to be lodged at Newgate or any other of her Majesty's places of detention." With which he turned about and into his bedroom and closed the door behind him.

"Mr. Allen," says I, "this man strikes me as a nimble enough fellow. Perhaps you had better be with him while he puts on his ruffles and wig."

"You might have observed, Mr. Creech," says he, "that we are located in the second storey of the house and that Mr. DeFoe's bedroom window leads to the rear where the constable is stationed."

Nevertheless, he knocked at the door and pushed the knob, but the door refused to give. "Mr. DeFoe!" says he.

"I shall be with you presently," says Mr. DeFoe, from behind the door, while downstairs his wife and children wailed and cried and comported themselves as though their provider had never before been off to gaol.

"Pray, Mr. DeFoe," says Mr. Allen, "will you open that door."

At that, there was a crash outside the house, and an outcry, and hurried steps, and the beat of hooves. I rushed down the stairs and wanted out, but the woman and her children clung to my knees and tore at my sleeves and wept and pleaded, "Mercy, sir, mercy on the poor orphans!" And before I could rid myself of the obstruction, the hoof beats had faded and the constable entered, one eye closed and his face mauled. "Why, Mr. Creech," says he at my query, "'tis a regular devil, your Mr. Ffooe. He plummets from the window, square on to my head, flattening me to the ground where I lie, numbed and spattered, and my sword here and my pistol there, and while I'm still trying to gather myself and my possessions, he cuts loose the horses and jumps on the fastest of them and is off to the woods."

Meanwhile, Mr. Allen descended and, finding the constable thus ill-used and our transport gone and the prisoner fled, fell to cursing. The woman and her children were again at my knees, tearfully imploring me.

"Madame," says I, "my Lord, the Earl of Nottingham, is a great patron of contemporary literature, and he and your husband would doubtlessly come upon many points of common interest. 'Twould therefore be to your favour and that of your little ones if you found the means of prevailing on your husband to give himself over to my Lord as soon as convenient. . . ."

January 5, 1703

. . . Mr. DeFoe's having made his escape from Mr. Allen and myself caused my Lord to take a more jaundiced view than ever of the affairs of the Kingdom. "'Tis your fault as well, Mr. Creech," says he, "for disregarding your superior's warning. Haven't I told you that literature and sedition are as one in this age, two sides of the coin which buys nothing but trouble, and that I have reason to suspect Mr. Ffooe of being not a mere purveyor of ambiguous words but, rather, the hub of a conspiracy."

At which a servant entering informed my Lord that the lady who had pleaded to be heard had arrived and was awaiting my Lord's pleasure.

So I went and escorted Mrs. DeFoe into my Lord's presence. She bent her knee, and my Lord bade her sit down, which after some hesitation she did, appearing frightened and faint, her carriage and face like an old woman's, though she was by several years younger than her husband.

"Pray, Madame," says my Lord, "state your business."

"'Tis that Mr. DeFoe is an innocent man and a loyal subject of her Majesty," says she, "who never for a moment thought of committing high crimes and misdemeanours, with his pen or otherwise, and who only desires peacefully to pursue his business and provide for his wife and numerous children." With this, the tears came shooting to her eyes and rolled down her cheeks, leaving tracks in the white powder she had spread on them to cover their blemishes.

"If your husband is as innocent as all that, Madame," says my Lord, "how is it that he keeps himself hidden from the authorities, and that you will not tell us his whereabouts? For I take it, Madame, that you did not venture to Whitehall at your own behest only, but undertook your petition at some instruction from your husband."

The woman once more fell to weeping and swore her request to be heard by my Lord was purely her own doing and that she knew not in the least where Mr. DeFoe was keeping himself, but that he would not have thought of hiding from the authorities if it weren't that he was frightened by what some of the Government's agents had told him of his prospects. "Though of lowly descent and a butcher's son," says she, "Mr. DeFoe rose to become a friend of the late King William, who was pleased to listen to his advice; Mr. DeFoe is a gentleman and could not bear the treatment threatened."

My Lord Nottingham replied that Mr. Ffooe was to answer certain questions and that his treatment depended on whether and how he answered these. "Make no mistake, however, Madame," says he, "as to the ability of her Majesty's Government to produce him. At this very hour, Madame, several of the Queen's messengers, assisted by constables and every manner of armed men, are scouring city and country, and neither Whitefriars nor the Mint nor any place of sanctuary will save your husband from the reach of the law, as Mr. Creech here will be glad to confirm."

"Why, Madame," says I, "'tis a hopeless thing indeed. The net's out and we'll have the fish; let him thresh a while, but to no avail; why not think of your children? The best service you can do your husband is to tell him to surrender or inform his Lordship where he may be found. His Lordship, I'm sure, wishes him no ill, and has the ear of her Majesty, and his word may make the difference between the cart's tail or the pillory for your husband and a few pounds' fine."

'Twas plain that the woman was weighing my words and was of a half mind to disclose her secret; but my Lord's impatience got the better of him and he harangued against conspirators and Dissenters, perhaps hoping to daunt the woman into owning what she knew. But though he sounded nearly like a page from her husband's pamphlet, all he got for his labour was another freshet of tears.

"Mr. Creech," says he finally, "have the person removed."

"May it please your Lordship," says I, "but it seems to me the woman will respond better to kindness." And turning to her, "Dry your tears, Madame," says I, "you have a friend in me, since I was much taken by you and your children the other night when Mr. DeFoe chose to leave you to your own resources. If my Lord has hurt you, 'tis because he has strong views on the duties of a loving subject of her Majesty. He does not know you, Madame, as I do. He does not know that you remained true to your husband even though he wasted every last penny of your dowry, all of three and a half thousand pounds, before he escaped his creditors, absconding to Bristol and appearing there every Sunday, bewigged and bejewelled and a wench on either arm, while you were begging a crust of bread for your children from the baker and pleading with the landlords for a poor roof over their innocent heads. My Lord does not know that you continued a good wife to Mr. DeFoe though he publicly flaunted that oyster girl, Mistress Norton, and made the wench with child, christening the bastard Benjamin, same name as one of your own children. My Lord does not know all this, else he would have told you that such a man is not worth the suffering you take upon yourself, Madame, and which you will be inflicting on those poor little ones who clung to my knees and implored me to protect them against a merciless fate."

Having dried her eyes, as I told her to do, the woman had been gazing at me steadfastly and towards the end with some amazement. Then, rising up, "Mr. Creech," says she, "you are a worse scoundrel than I thought," and to my Lord, "your Lordship, I deeply regret having presumed on your time," and bent her knee and retired. . . .

January 8, 1703

. . . so I once more to Robin Hog, after arranging to have the woman followed and the house at Tilbury watched, and having word passed to diverse well-meaning citizens to be on the lookout for our man.

Mr. Stephens was gone out, his servant woman told me, but would be back presently.

"Gone out! Why," says I, "he was in bed but recently, unable to move from the gout."

"'Twas a miracle indeed," says she. "Between Christmas and New Year's some gentlemen in the publishing business presented my master with a half side of beef, a basketful of oysters, and a barrel of wine, in acknowledgement of past favours, they said; and though I warned him to spare his feeble body, he went at the victuals like a starved soldier, saying there's no better medicine for what ails a person than a double portion of what struck him. So he gorged and guzzled for three days, with hardly a pause for sleep, and on New Year's morn he rose without an ache in his foot or anywhere on him, but his girth greatly enlarged, and whistled and pranced about, and now he is gone out, says he, to see about a bird."

I waited, then, for nearly an hour, when Mr. Hog returned, sighing pitiably, his clothes dirtied and muddy, his foot as unwieldy as ever.

"Have you had a relapse, Mr. Stephens," says I, "after so encouraging a progress?"

"Relapse!" says he. "Why, Mr. Creech, I'm as good as dead."

"Who killed you?" says I.

"Your Mr. Ffooe," says he.

"Have you seen him?" says I.

"As I am seeing you at this present moment, Mr. Creech," says he. "And more closely."

"Then why, pray, did you not bring him with you?" says I. "You might have taken him by virtue of your commission as a Queen's messenger, or, a warrant being out for him, simply by virtue of your being a loyal subject of her Majesty."

"'Tis no doubt that I would have, Mr. Creech," says he, "but for that unfortunate foot of mine. I was walking in Hackney Field, at the vague information of a person whose name is of no import, when I spied coming towards me a man in every appearance familiar, with lively dark eyes, hooked nose, sharp chin, and sallow-complexioned, the man looking neither right nor left but seemingly deep in thought. Here, Robin, says I to myself, is a true piece of luck, not a second face like this one in all of England since the demise of the late King William; and though I could not discern a soul within hailing distance if help were needed, I stopped the man, lifting my hat, and greeting, 'The great author of *The True-Born Englishman*, if I am not deceived, Mr. Daniel Ffooe!' 'Why, Mr. Hog,' says he, lifting his hat civilly enough, 'what strange wind blew you along?' 'A wind of good chance,' says I. ''Tis a happy wind indeed that blows together old friends; you will accompany me, I hope; there's a gentleman in high places who wishes to talk with you about literature and allied subjects.' 'The pillory,' says he, 'stands on a high place; so does the gibbet. If you forgive me, I will go on my own way.' At this I took hold of him, but he drew, and before I could draw the toothache was back in my foot and I went down on my knee, while Mr Ffooe gave me a near shave with his blade. Then, placing the tip of his sword to my throat, he inquired, 'Is your mother alive, Mr. Hog?' 'No, sir,' says I, 'she's gone these many years.' 'That makes it a problem,' says he, 'since your honour is nothing a person would wish to swear by.' 'I could swear by my life,' says I, 'if you would let me.' 'Your life isn't worth much,' says he. 'To me, having only one life, it's worth a great deal,' says I. 'The value of an object is in its scarcity.' 'I was brought up a merchant,' says he, 'I appreciate your argument. Swear then, Mr. Hog, that if ever you meet me again, you will shut your eyes till I am half a mile off you.' 'I will, Mr. Ffooe,' says I, 'by my life. And now, if you could remove that thing from my Adam's apple, 'tis an uncommonly raw day and the cold point makes me shiver.' 'Well, Mr. Hog,' says he, 'then shut your eyes.' Which I did, feeling the stab of ice at my throat for a long time, and the toothache in my foot. When I dared rise and look about me I found neither hair nor hide of him, just a few passers-by staring at me as though I had sprung from Bedlam."

"Let me congratulate you, Mr. Stephens," says I, "on your presence of mind, by which you no doubt averted a worse fate than which befell you."

"Mr. Creech," says he, "I am moved. But I am certain, had you been in my place, you would have conducted yourself no less creditably. . . ."

January 10, 1703

. . . another wretched day. "The man you were to have caught some while ago, Mr. Creech," says my Lord, "has communicated with us."

"May I inquire from your Lordship, how?" says I. "And from where?"

"From London," says he, "by ordinary penny post." He gazed at me with an expression at once so haughty and so full of gloom that I could understand the vicious pamphleteer who once lampooned him as *Don Dismal*. "I strongly fear," says he, "that you will never take Mr. Ffooe unless he walks directly into Whitehall, and even then you and Mr. Stephens might shut your eyes till he's walked out again, having bit his thumb at her Majesty's Government."

"Your Lordship's judgement seems too harsh," says I. "Her Majesty's servants in this Department are conducting themselves with wisdom and circumspection. 'Tis like a whale hunt: the beast may keep under water for a time, but in the end he must come up and blow."

"I wish your actions were as apt as your images, Mr. Creech," says he. "Here's the letter; see what you conclude from it."

The letter was written on cheap stock, with bad ink, and in haste; but the words were well chosen and well reasoned; hard-pressed though he was the man wrote well.

"'Tis obvious, your Lordship," says I, "that Mr. DeFoe feels ill at ease in his present circumstances. *To flee from her Majesty's justice is very irksome to me*, he writes, and he beseeches you *for a truce*, and worries at his *body being unfit to bear the hardships of prison* and his *mind impatient of confinement*, at *the cries of a numerous ruined family, and the prospect of a long banishment from my native country*. This all presages success."

"Does it, Mr. Creech?" says he, beckoning me to return the letter to his hand. "From what I read, it seems that his fears, if any, are far surpassed by his impudence. And why should he feel differently? Although you are having his wife watched, Mr. Creech, he easily communicates with her, for I find him writing here: *when my distressed wife made application to your Lordship, you were pleased to direct that I should surrender and answer such questions as should be asked me.* And he goes on to demand, we should have these questions *writ down and sent to, or left at, his house,* and he would deign *to answer them as soon as he can receive them.* He not only ridicules us, he poses conditions! And to top his insolence, he offers a barter. If we spare him *the rigour of prosecution,* he writes, and agree to giving him a sentence *a little more tolerable to him as a gentleman than prisons, pillories, and such like,* he will surrender himself *to any colonel of horse* of her Majesty's *armies in the Netherlands* and *die there much more to her Majesty's service than in a prison.*"

My Lord turned up his eyes. "Listen to this, Mr. Creech; 'tis Mr. Ffooe's highest bid: *But if her Majesty shall extend her grace to a total remission of my offence, I will raise her Majesty a troop of horse, at my own charges, and at the head of them I'll serve her as long as I live*. . . . And has the effrontery to sign, *Your most obedient, distressed, humble petitioner and servant.*"

"We frequently stick highwaymen, pirates, thieves, or rapists into the army," says I. "'Tis more economical than hanging them."

"An army of felons, Mr. Creech," says he, "is no threat to established order. But a rebellious writer belongs safely locked in Newgate, and I advise you, Mr. Creech, to get him there as fast as you can."

"And what will your Lordship reply to the letter?" says I.

"Why, Mr. Creech," says he, "we'll answer it publicly. Will you note this and cause it to be inserted in the next issue of the *London Gazette.*" My Lord paused, and then dictated, "*St. James's,* today's date. *Whereas Daniel Ffooe* alias et cetera *is charged with writing a scandalous and seditious pamphlet entitled 'The Shortest Way with the Dissenters,' whoever shall discover the said Daniel Ffooe to one of her Majesty's Principal Secretaries of State or any of her Majesty's Justices of the Peace, so as he may be apprehended, shall have a reward of fifty pounds which her Majesty has ordered immediately to be paid on such discovery.*"

This generosity from my Lord, otherwise one of the stingiest of men, struck me as truly remarkable. . . .

January 16, 1703

. . . had Mr. George Croome, the printer, taken to Newgate.

Upon being informed of this, "'Tis hardly likely," says my Lord, "that Mr. Ffooe would come forth to relieve his printer. His own skin is what's closest to a man, and since Christ dying on the Cross to save among others you, Mr. Creech, few men indeed have ventured on a like course. However, the surest way to control the printing press is to put away the printer; therefore something useful will be achieved at all events. . . ."

January 25, 1703

. . . my Lord let on that Lord Godolphin has set aside, out of treasury funds, two hundred pounds for the prosecution in *The Queen against DeFoe and others for a libel entitled "The Shortest Way with the Dissenters."* At my remarking that we were paying half the informers of London and several elsewhere, aside from employing diverse Queen's messengers, constables, and other officials to assist in the search for Mr. DeFoe, my Lord allayed my fears by assuring me that treasury was defraying legal expenses only; other costs would be covered by a special appropriation out of secret service. . . .

February 1, 1703

. . . after a leisurely breakfast to Justice Hall in Old Bailey where, in sessions of Oyer and Terminer, the indictment was to be brought against Daniel DeFoe.

The court, presided over by the Lord Mayor, was composed of the highest-ranking jurists, among them the Chief Justice, Sir John Holt, and others whose tails Mr. DeFoe had twisted in past pamphlets and pasquils. There was considerable craning of heads and querying by the public if Mr. DeFoe might turn up. When it was plain that he would not, Mr. Chief Justice opened and the indictment was read stating that seventeen honest and lawful men of the City of London had sworn that on December 22, 1702, copies of a libel entitled *The Shortest Way with the Dissenters* was offered for sale in the Parish of Bow in the Ward of Cheap and alleging that said libel, authorised by the defendant, sought to keep the Protestant Dissenters from enjoying the religious toleration granted them by Royal Act of 1689.

'Twas an ingenious artifice upon which Solicitor General Harcourt had come. He could not very well prosecute Mr. DeFoe for following the High Clergy's own thought to its logical conclusion and thereby reducing fine Christian words to absurdity and making dangerous fools of men high in positions of power. Thus the Solicitor-General pretended DeFoe's irony to be his earnest and took the mock accusations hurled at the Dissenters and the high-flying threats delivered against them at face value, and so charged the satirist with propounding what those he satirised wished in their heart's heart but dared not utter. 'Twas as though a person straight-facedly claimed the cuckoo's egg in the thrush's nest in truth to be the thrush's and proceeded to accuse the cuckoo of having laid a thrush's egg.

In the absence of the defendant, however, the case had to be adjourned, and the justices commanded the Sheriff of London to bring Daniel DeFoe before them at the next session of Oyer and Terminer, viz., on April 7, 1703, in Old Bailey. . . .

February 26, 1703

. . . concurrent with the proceedings in court, my Lord had arranged for a complaint to be made in the House of Commons, which promptly ordered the public burning of the seditious and malicious libel *The Shortest Way with the Dissenters*.

So I, early in the morning, to New Palace Yard, Westminster, my Lord desiring me to relate to him the general mood and any undue incidents at the event. I found the crowd quiet, at times subdued, except for some drunken ruffians who would cheer at anything and a few clergy who applauded as the public hangman stepped forth and put the torch to a goodly pile of the treacherous papers.

These burned well, the smoke rising steeply to a clear, cold sky.

One man, a minister of the Church with a face full of pustles, called out, "Wish to God 'twas this Ffooe burning on top of his books"; but another said, "Do you believe, sir, that 'tis as simple as that, you burn the books and you burn the man, and his ideas are thrown to the wind along with the ashes?"

Afterwards, the hangman joined me in a tavern near by. "Mr. Creech," says he, "pray let us have more book burnings. They're a minor item, financially, but many small make a great and we are grateful for anything."

"You're in luck, Friend," says I. "Her Majesty, in her constant concern for her loving subjects, may say a word or two on your plea when Parliament convenes tomorrow."

"Why, Mr. Creech," says he, admiringly, "you're a true man of miracles." But 'twas simply that my Lord Nottingham was favoured with having to draft that section of the Queen's speech, and the scribe had shown me a copy of his paper, my Lord having phrased it most prettily, viz., *I think it might have been for the public service to have had some further laws for restraining the great licence which is assumed of publishing and spreading scandalous pamphlets and libels; but as far as the present laws extend, I hope you will all do your duty, in your respective stations, to prevent and punish such pernicious practices.*

So my promise to the hangman was well-founded, and he felt most encouraged, and in anticipation of his hoped-for prosperity paid for the wine and the oysters. . . .

March 15, 1703

. . . it seems that it's no longer the cat playing with the mouse but *vice versa*. Today Mr. Hog brought me a pamphlet fresh off the presses, wheezing excitedly, "'Tis all over the city, in the book-stalls, and being hawked at the corners. A Phoenix risen from the ashes, Mr. Creech, a new edition of *The Shortest Way with the Dissenters* with a new foreword by the author."

I read the foreword for any useful hints it might contain; there were none, except one saw it as proof of a plucky nature. Being hunted and forced into hiding, Mr. DeFoe had lost none of his wit and his mastery of the double meaning; he took back with one word what he conceded with the other, and offered us one more trade, viz., *if the people now in trouble be excused, to throw himself upon the favour of the Government rather than others should be ruined for his mistakes.*

"Mr. Creech," says Robin Hog, helping himself to the sausage and beer my landlady had carried in for me to breakfast on, "I gravely fear for your position. Not only has Mr. Ffooe escaped you all this while, but he has leisurely authored new mischief, found a printer, corrected proof, transacted business with numerous people, and all this while you have an army of spies lying in wait for him."

"You forget, Mr. Stephens," says I, "that England is blessed with an orderly Government, where each peg has its hole and each man his competency, and yours is the press."

Whereupon Mr. Hog pulled from his pocket a smudged paper, an attestation from his doctor, stating that Robert Stephens, Esquire, was severely afflicted by the gout, also by lumbago, febrility, miasma, rheum, dyspepsia, as well as varicose veins and haemorrhoids, and thus was for the present incapable of fulfilling the diverse duties assigned him and should be excused from same.

"Well then, Mr. Stephens," says I, "may I count at least on your experience and advice?"

"If it's the printer you want me to identify, Mr. Creech," says he, "'tis not possible this time, the job having been done with extreme care to disguise the origin of typeface and paper."

"'Tis not the printer of this edition I want, Mr. Stephens," says I. "I want another one, to do some work for me, and I want the most unconscionable, greediest man in the business."

"Try John How," says he. "There's no greater rogue that ever inked a line of type and placed it under the press. . . ."

April 7, 1703

. . . back again at Old Bailey to hear the Court once more adjourn the case of *The Queen against Daniel DeFoe and others*, the Sheriff of London having testified to his inability to produce the defendant.

Then to my Lord, who with a countenance dark and doleful remarked on the imperfection of Man in general and mine in particular and inquired how long I thought we could keep the Court in abeyance and when I expected to have Mr. Ffooe available to be questioned and disposed of?

"Within six weeks," says I.

"How so, Mr. Creech?" says he, with a brief gleam in his eyes. "Has the whale been coming up for air?"

"We've shot off a harpoon," says I, "and we hope it will stick."

"That it better had, Mr. Creech," says he, cracking the joints of his long fingers. "The ruin of his brick works, the straits in which his family finds itself, and various other predicaments have failed to produce him. What manner of harpoon is it you have shot off?"

At this, I placed a parcel upon my Lord's desk and untied it for him, saying, "A modest present to your Lordship, with the compliments of the printer, Mr. John How."

My Lord frowned at the volumes, holding them in his hand much as he would a poisonous spider.

"*The Collected Writings of Daniel DeFoe*," says I, "including *The*

Shortest Way with the Dissenters, at two shillings and six. A fair edition, your Lordship will agree, as well printed and nicely bound as hurry permitted. But aside from these qualities it possesses one which will surely entice the author to where we can lay hands upon him."

"Which would that be?" says my Lord doubtfully.

"It's pirated," says I. . . .

May 21, 1703

. . . on May 12 another session of Oyer and Terminer was concluded at Old Bailey without Mr. DeFoe having been produced to hear his indictment and answer charges. My Lord Nottingham grimly reminded me that I had but one week left of the six I had wanted. What with the anti-Dissenters bill being opposed in the Lords, and agitation rising in the coffee houses, and some men in high places coveting his position, my Lord was under pressure which even a more sanguine person than he would pass on to his subordinates.

But patience will bring its rewards. Some days ago, upon rumours of a plot being afoot to rise up, loot, burn, and plunder the rich, a general search for disaffected persons was conducted in Spittlefields. Along with the constables and soldiers were sent a number of informers who were to point out the leaders of the plot and those known for their refractoriness. Yesterday then, one Lemuel Finney, a disreputable individual blind in one eye and stinking, was brought to me by Mr. Dagley, Queen's Messenger in ordinary, who said that the man had something to tell which he would disclose only to one of her Majesty's principal Secretaries of State, and under certain guarantees.

"Well, Finney," says I, "I fear his Lordship will not receive you in your present unwashed state, and I take it you are interested in more tangible advantages than being scrubbed and deterged and prettied up. Furthermore, I happen to be his Lordship's confidential agent and adviser, aide and adjunct, and talking to me is as good as talking to him, and what is it you wish to have guaranteed?"

At this, the fellow fished from his pocket a much creased page torn from the *London Gazette* and laid it before me and inquired if the promise of fifty pounds for the discovery of Daniel Ffooe to one of her Majesty's principal Secretaries of State still held true. I warranted it did, whereupon he said he was one of the men who had helped the authorities, for a slight fee, in the selection of suspects to be lodged in Newgate, these past days, and in so doing had come upon the house of one Sammen, a Frenchman and weaver, in Spittlefields, which they searched, and that he had observed there a well-dressed gentleman who sat at a table, immersed in his writing, and who fit the description printed in the *Gazette* to the wart on his chin. The fellow avowed that he had disclosed his secret to no one but me so he would not be impelled to share his reward with any constable or other officers; he preferred being paid on the spot; he begged us to keep his name and person secret, for fear some friend of Mr. DeFoe's might want to stick a knife in him.

"You may set your mind at ease, Finney," says I. "There isn't a Government in the world that would betray its informers, for without them the mightiest Ministers would be deaf and blind and at the mercy of the populace, and your payment will be forthcoming upon the capture of Mr. DeFoe."

I then requested Mr. Dagley to meet me at midnight, together with Mr. Allen who was to have with him the warrant my Lord had issued, and to secure the services of half a dozen constables, all young, agile men able to use their weapons.

At midnight we set out and arrived in due time in Spittlefields and, one of the constables previously having searched the place, soon found the house of the French weaver, Sammen. But for a dog barking noisily, we were unnoticed and surrounded the house on all sides, after which Mr. Allen knocked at the door and demanded access in the name of her Majesty. 'Twas a small house,

Mr. Sammen being a poor man, with one back room from which Mr. DeFoe emerged, not in the least surprised, and surrendered himself to Mr. Allen and Mr. Dagley, saying he had expected us.

"How so?" says I. "And if you expected us, why didn't you flee in good time, as you have done these past four and a half months, and hide elsewhere?"

"Why, Mr. Creech," says he, looking at me from his sharp eyes, "I had a dream, several nights ago, in which I saw you and these two gentlemen as clearly as I am seeing you now, including the arms you carry and the hats you wear and your buckles and belts, and you were entering and laying your hands upon me. I swear this is true; I have told my brother-in-law of it, and he advised me to leave the city post haste, but I wouldn't."

"Because of the power of the dream," says I, "or because of Mr. How, the printer?"

He once more looked at me strangely, but did not speak, and held out his wrists to be tied. . . .

May 22, 1703

. . . had the prisoner brought before my Lord Nottingham at Whitehall. My Lord and Mr. DeFoe took an immediate dislike to one another; and truly there could be no greater contrast than between these two: the one gaunt, dour, misanthropic; the other short and sinewy, facetious, and at pains to douse his sparkle so as not unnecessarily to vex his inquisitor.

"Now that we have you, Mr. Ffooe," says my Lord, "I can hold out only one hope for you, viz., to confess all and throw yourself upon the mercy of the Queen. You will not deny, I presume, that you are the author of the libel entitled *The Shortest Way with the Dissenters*?"

To which Mr. DeFoe replied that he had written the booklet, but intending no ill, and that he was misinterpreted and misunderstood as, unfortunately, had been many authors in history from Socrates on down.

My Lord countered that he was not concerned with the case of *The Government of Athens against Socrates*, its facts having been thoroughly shrouded by Plato, but with *The Queen against Daniel Ffooe*, in which the facts were clear and present and undeniable, the corpus delicti being as malicious and factious a pamphlet as ever had incurred the displeasure of her Majesty, and that Mr. Ffooe had done the nation an ill office by authoring such a scandalous libel and causing it to be printed.

"Your Lordship," says Mr. DeFoe in a voice sweetly persuasive, "if I had known the offence this small work would induce in high places, I would rather have hacked off my hand than put it to the manuscript." But 'twas plain from the set of his lips and the glow of his eyes that he was secretly proud of the effects of his thought and enjoying the eminence his words had brought him, even though it was fraught with danger.

"Mr. Ffooe," says my Lord, "I should like to mention that your prevarications vainly consume our time and do not help us. 'Tis obvious to any knowledgeable person that a man of your history and metier does not proceed on his own account, particularly not in an action involving such grave risk, and that others, keeping in the background, put him up to it. If you name these, Mr. Ffooe, I will pledge my word that the Court will let you off with a nominal punishment; otherwise it's the pillory, and Mr. Creech here will see to it that the rotten fish and the brickbats hit their target."

At this, Mr. DeFoe paled and a weakness befell his knees; so I placed a chair near him, and with my Lord's permission he sat down on it and after a while recovered his voice. "I shall endeavour to explain to your Lordship," says he, "how a writer's mind, or my mind at least, functions, so your Lordship will perceive that there is no one in the background and no conspiracy, but only a man with his thought and his pen."

My Lord Nottingham folded his long fingers and leaned back with a sneer, but said nothing.

"'Tis like a bolt from the blue," says Mr. DeFoe, "which lights a flame, and nothing will quench the fire until it has burned its course through field and woods. Or like an itch that will not cease until the blood flows from your scratching."

"What bolt?" says my Lord. "Which itch? Precisely, pray."

"The idea."

My Lord's countenance darkened as he thought he was being derided, but Mr. DeFoe, being concentrated on his theme, failed to notice.

"I read the sermon of Dr. Sacheverell and other such zealots," says the prisoner, "I was treated to the arguments of sinister idiots hankering after a bigoted past, and suddenly I thought I heard the glorious laughter of the late King William, whom I had the honour to serve, and the echo of the revolution, which I had the honour to fight for, and I saw that all I need do was fully to state the case of the established numskulls to have it drowned in ridicule."

"Why, Mr. Ffooe," says my Lord, swallowing hard, "you do not believe that I will be satisfied with such fellow conspirators as the ghost of a dead King and the echo of a revolution?"

It was now the turn of Mr. DeFoe to swallow, for he realised that in his ardour to convince my Lord of the pamphlet being exclusively his enterprise, he had neglected the possibility that my Lord would count himself among the sinister idiots and established numskulls. "I humbly beg your Lordship's pardon," says he, "if in an endeavour to shed some light on the influences that move an author's mind I have expressed myself with undue passion. However, I have been pursued for over four months by your Lordship's agents, my business is ruined, my wife hard pressed by creditors, my children want for the amenities. I must make myself clear to your Lordship, for I'm an honest man and will suffer rather than falsely accuse other people."

'Twould have been a profitable plea but for the person to whom it was addressed. My Lord Nottingham was a man cool to the root of his heart and, once having decided on a notion, stubborn as a donkey. To him, Mr. DeFoe was not merely a writer and satirist, a doubter of authority and subverter of established order, in short, the devil in the flesh, but also the keystone of a plot by which he felt himself threatened.

"Well, Mr. Ffooe," says he, "I take it, then, that presently you are in no mood to talk further and unburden yourself so as to enable me to ease your condition?"

"I have told your Lordship all there is to tell," says the prisoner. "I beg of you to consider that I am in no sense a criminal, and that I have hid from the law only because of the inordinate threats made against me by your Lordship's agents and repeated today, in no uncertain terms, by your Lordship himself."

"Mr. Creech," says my Lord, "will you commit this man close prisoner to Newgate, there to be kept in safe custody till he is discharged by due course of law. Have him conveyed in a coach, and under armed guard, for there is reason to assume that some of his fellows may attempt to snatch him away from us. And, Mr. Creech," adds he, "will you have the keeper instructed that the prisoner is to be brought to me at any time, day or night, upon his signifying that he is prepared to make a statement."

Mr. Dagley and Mr. Allen being available, I had them escort Mr. DeFoe to Newgate, where he was lodged in a small cell that could be securely locked. I thereupon devoted myself to sorting and reading the many papers and libels found in his room upon his arrest. Few were of interest except a manuscript wherein he queried if her Majesty Queen Anne, by succeeding King William, was not as much of an usurper as the late King. And not a line anywhere would serve to prove a plot or point up the plotters. . . .

June 1, 1703

. . . the Lord Treasurer, Lord Godolphin, having furnished out of secret service monies the fifty pounds promised for the discovery of Mr DeFoe, I paid Lemuel Finney who, after acknowledging the receipt by his mark, kissed my hand and swore he would forever be my friend and servant. As he pocketed the purse and was about to retire, I recalled him to warn that now that he was rich he was in danger of being waylaid, and deprived of his bounty, and losing his life to boot.

"Why, Mr. Creech," says he, "no one but you and Mr. Dagley know who put the finger on Mr. Ffooe, and you are the only one to know that I was paid the reward."

At this I praised him for a sharp mind to have noticed that particular, and encouraged him to draw his conclusions, which he quickly did, winking his one eye and dropping half the purse on a tin plate conveniently placed near him, for the benefit of the Queen and her excellent servants, he said.

I then drove to Newgate and, having the prisoner bound over to me, took him once more to Whitehall where he was to be heard before the Privy Council. Mr. DeFoe said little on the way, but for inquiring where I was bringing him and why. Lack of exercise and fresh air, and scarce nourishment, had lent him that pallor commonly found on men and women in Newgate; however, he had kept himself fairly clean and I could detect no lice or other vermin on him.

We waited a considerable while before being led into the presence of the Council, which was composed of my Lord Nottingham; the Lord Treasurer, Lord Godolphin; the Lord Privy Seal, the Duke of Buckinghamshire and Normanby; and other great lords and gentlemen, all seated and regarding Mr. DeFoe with slight interest and as though he were keeping them from their dinner, which he probably was. My Lord Nottingham introduced the prisoner as the author of that vicious libel, subversive of Church and Government. *The Shortest Way with the Dissenters*, and other pamphlets and writings, most of them equally ill-intentioned and doubtful. Turning to Mr. DeFoe, then, he said that none the less it was the sense of the Privy Council that the prisoner should be given this opportunity to explain himself and to state why and at whose prodding and purpose he published so malicious and factious a pamphlet; further that, if he showed contrition and an open heart and named the set of men who employed him and with whom he had plotted, he would be dealt with leniently and as a gentleman; otherwise the full severity of the law would be applied against him, and none of his fellow conspirators, high-placed or low-placed, whom he sought to protect by his silence, would be able or willing to protect him.

Mr. DeFoe was plainly perturbed, not so much, I believe, by the titled personages he was facing as by my Lord Nottingham's stipulation. He allowed, respectfully addressing the Council, that his work *The Shortest Way with the Dissenters* might be ill-conceived and ill-timed and open to misunderstanding, but that their Lordships would be hard put to prove a crime in his saying in jest what others had said in earnest, and that for so slight a legerdemain he truly would not need to conspire with anyone but a printer, the conspiracy consisting in the act of transmitting the manuscript.

But he did not deny, said Lord Privy Seal, narrowly gazing at the prisoner, that he had written the piece for a political purpose, viz., to influence her Majesty's subjects?

"There isn't an author in England, your Lordship," says Mr. DeFoe, "who doesn't write with the same purpose in mind, and if you make that a crime, you will soon have every writer hanging from the gallows."

To which Lord Godolphin, who was this day plagued by the gout, observed that considering the vexations caused by writers, her Majesty's Government could do worse than dispose of them in this manner. Lord Privy Seal suggested that buying them would be more expedient, for they certainly could be utilised to propound her Majesty's views to the general public. This annoyed my Lord Nottingham who turned on Lord Privy Seal, saying, "Does not your Lordship realise that this man *is* bought, and that we're attempting to elicit who employed him and for what aim?"

"Well, Mr. Ffooe," says Lord Privy Seal, "the Lord Treasurer will match anything you were paid and half over; how is it, be a good fellow, take the offer and let us finish with this."

Mr. DeFoe could have named his own price. He was plucked from dungeon, penniless; we had ruined his business and driven his family to penury. I saw him chewing on his lip; 'tis a terrible temptation: money, and freedom, and safety.

"I wish I could accept your Lordship's kindness," says he finally. "But I fear you would not receive value for your price."

"How so?" says Lord Privy Seal, the Duke of Buckinghamshire and Normanby. "You would not willingly give us short measure?"

"The tailor will cut the suit to fit his cutomer," says the prisoner, "but words, though lighter than any cloth, refuse to be so treated. Their texture is not of sheep's hair or of some worm's excretion; they breathe the life the author has breathed into them by the fervour of his heart; without that, they're a dead shell and no one the wiser for them."

"Your fervour then, Mr. Ffooe," says my Lord Nottingham, "will blow only one way—against her Majesty?"

"Why, no," says the prisoner, "I deny this."

"Against whom else?" says my Lord.

"Against hypocrisy," says the prisoner, "against injustice and intolerance."

At this Lord Godolphin, who was in pain, turned to my Lord Nottingham, inquiring, "I'm sure your Lordship has not brought this man before us so he might display the nobility of his sentiments, but to enlighten us on the origins of as outrageous a piece of demagogy as was perpetrated within recent years?"

My Lord Nottingham confirmed this, adding that the prisoner, though given every opportunity to improve his situation, had shown himself hardened and that the law would now take its course. . . .

July 7, 1703

. . . in sessions of Oyer and Terminer, at Old Bailey, the court being crowded with spectators: journalists, clergymen, idlers from the coffee houses, doubtful folk, and gentlemen of rank, among them diverse members of the House; all animated and expectant, the bets standing two to one against Mr. DeFoe appearing, on the assumption that he would forfeit his fifteen hundred pounds bail rather than the pillory.

Granting of bail and setting it at the extraordinary amount of £1,500 was my Lord Nottingham's doing. Keep an eye on him, Mr. Creech, he said, we shall see who furnishes his bond and whose aid he solicits; thus we might find the end of the thread from which to unravel the web; also call upon one Mr. Colepeper who has agreed to defend Mr. Ffooe at the bar; find out his mind as to his prevailing on Mr. Ffooe to plead guilty; do not pledge but hint broadly that we would treat Mr. Ffooe tenderly if he so pleads.

A scrutiny of the bondsmen led nowhere. They were small people, a shipwright, a baker, a broker, and such, each contributing his savings and capital laid by—Mr. DeFoe bringing in the largest share, viz., £500, borrowed through his wife's brother. Nor did he, between his release from Newgate and the day of the trial, consort with any likely plotters. He dealt with a printer for another edition, duly authorised, of his collected writings, and for the rest occupied himself trying to rescue his business and attend to his impaired exchequer. As to why he would not run from his bail, though plainly frightened of being crippled or killed in the pillory, he told a friend who warned him in the words of the disciple, *Master, save thyself*, that several of his bondsmen had pressed him to go away and given him their free consent; but the reputation of his integrity and the justice of the cause he was embarked in prevented him from doing so. By that time, however, I had spoken to Mr. Colepeper, who was the most eager to clutch the straw I held out and who in all sincerity heard from my words just what he desired to hear, adding *b* and *c* to my half *a*, without in any way probing for the Government's real intent or demanding a firm commitment. A good attorney experienced in public trials would scarce have risked placing his client at the mercy of the court; but Mr. Colepeper was a country gentleman, slightly acquainted with the law, who upon hearing that Mr. DeFoe was unable to employ expert counsel offered his services out of gratitude, a previous pamphlet by Mr. DeFoe having been instrumental in freeing him from gaol.

When, therefore, at ten sharp the defendant appeared with Mr. Colepeper and took his seat in the dock, a great buzz followed and lasted until the entry of the court. The Lord Mayor, Sir Samuel Dashwood, opened proceedings, and the Chief Justice, Sir John Holt, caused the indictment to be read once again, the defendant having been absent at its first reading in the session of February 24. Then he asked in a loud voice, "Mr. Ffooe, do you plead guilty to the charges as read?"

The indictment consisting in the main of quotes from *The Shortest Way with the Dissenters*, Mr. DeFoe had sat through it as one enrapt.

"Mr. Ffooe!" says Mr. Chief Justice.

Mr. DeFoe started. But before he could say Yes, sir, or No, Mr. Colepeper rose to declare that in the light of her Majesty's merciful mind and in view of certain other considerations, the defendant pleaded guilty.

"You do, Mr. Ffooe," says Mr. Chief Justice, "do you?"

Mr. DeFoe looked to his counsellor, who nodded emphatically, and then at the Chief Justice, and shrugged as one saying, what can I do.

At this, an even greater buzz arose among the spectators, and one said, "He's hung himself, poor fellow." The Lord Mayor called for order and then requested Solicitor General Harcourt to speak to the sentencing.

'Twas a case after the heart of Sir Simon Harcourt. If he had

had to prove his charges, he should have been hard put, especially against a good attorney; but now he had his victim prostrate, and lashed out unhampered and uninhibited, culminating his invective by claiming that *The Shortest Way* was paved with the skulls of Churchmen and would lead England to anarchy and civil war unless an example was made of its author.

By this time both Mr. DeFoe and his hapless lawyer must have known what position they had placed themselves in, Mr. DeFoe staring dejectedly at his knees, and Mr. Colepeper trying to gather his wits for a plea which at best would be a weak whine for mercy.

But no one among the spectators, except myself, expected the severity of the sentence as read by the Chief Justice, *for a fine of 200 marks of the lawful money of England, and to stand upon the pillory, one day in Cornhill by the Exchange, London, and another day in Cheapside near the Conduit there, the third day in Fleet Street by Temple Bar, for one hour between the hours of eleven before noon and two after noon, whichever one he likes, with a paper on his head on which his offences are written, and that the said Daniel Ffooe alias DeFoe should find good sureties to be of good behaviour for the space of seven years then next following.*

The hand of my Lord Nottingham showed in the fine touch of the prisoner being permitted to choose the hour of his infliction. My Lord had won, and while Mr. DeFoe was committed back to Newgate to be kept in the custody of the sheriffs of London, my Lord only need wait for the prisoner's spirit to break. . . .

July 19, 1703

. . . Mr. DeFoe was to stand in the pillory this date, but 'twas postponed, and most likely will be postponed again.

"Mr. Creech," says my Lord Nottingham the other day, "do you believe 'tis possible there is no plot?"

"Is there a doubt in your Lordship's mind?" says I.

"Not in mine," says he, "but other personages of great renown are having second thoughts and query if Mr. Ffooe might not have acted on his own, as he maintains, and if the court did not deal too severely with him, and if some of the public might not turn against us for it. 'Tis a strange thing about some people; they will pull strings but cry halt when the puppets begin to dance; in short, they would like mercy to be shown him; but how can we advocate mercy unless he confesses, and how can he confess unless there's a plot?"

"Plot or no plot," says I, "confessions are twelve to the dozen, and some men will throw in a thirteenth for the asking. 'Tis a question of how it is put to him and by whom."

"Mr. Creech?" says my Lord, with a leer.

"Not I," says I. "If your Lordship will recall, 'twas I who convinced Mr. Colepeper to have his client plead guilty."

"Perhaps we should pick one of his own," says my Lord, "a Dissenter, a minister of his Church if possible. The clergy regardless of shading can be quite persuasive, and is easily accessible."

"I think I should bring to your Lordship's attention," says I, "that the prisoner addressed himself from his dungeon to three of the most prominent dissenting ministers, desiring them to kneel beside him in prayer: and all three refused, although one of them some years ago did come to Newgate to pray with Mr. Whitney before the latter's hanging; but Mr. Whitney was a robber and murderer and not a writer with a mind of his own."

"I take it then," says my Lord, "that Mr. Ffooe is cast down and in great fear?"

"'Tis hard to determine," says I, "the reports of the keepers being at variance. Some find him deep in despondency, some in high hopes of divine or other intercession. Friends having supplied him with a small sum, he could pay for a single cell, bedding, candles, as well as food and drink, paper and pen, but he complains of the filth and the dankness, the clamour and noises, and the malodorous vapours which, he says, carry jail fever and other diseases. Nevertheless, he frequently seeks the company of fellow prisoners and cares not who they might be, highwaymen, thieves, sharpers, prostitutes, and closely listens to their stories. He writes and corrects previous writings for the printer and dispatches a number of letters. It has been observed that he is most composed, if not cheerful, when thus occupied."

At this, my Lord grew quite impatient, exclaiming at the humanity of her Majesty's Government; but then said he thought he had the right person to attend to the matter, viz. Mr. William Penn who, though a Quaker, was highly regarded at court and frequently employed by Lord Godolphin in carrying messages to people he did not think proper to converse with himself.

So I, with a letter from my Lord Nottingham, to Mr. William Penn, but found only William Penn, Jr., the elder Penn having left London for a day or two. Penn, Jr., who is reputed to be as dissolute a person as his father is abstemious and upright, took an interest in the matter. "Ah, Newgate," says he, "there's life for you, Mr. Creech, and Mr. DeFoe is a great wit. Why wait for my father? The case is urgent, his Lordship writes; I shall go in my father's stead and broach the proposal to the prisoner."

Which Mr. Penn, Jr., did, and with apparent success, and informed his father thereof. For my Lord received from Lord Godolphin a letter dated Windsor, July 17, which said in part, *After I had the honour to see your Lordship yesterday, Mr. William Penn came to me to tell me he had acquainted my Lord Privy Seal that DeFoe was ready to make oath to your Lordship of all that he knew, and to give an account of all his accomplices in whatsoever has been concerned, for the information of the Queen and the Lords of the Council, provided that by so doing he may be excused from the punishment of the pillory and not produced as an evidence against any person whatsoever.*

"Well, Mr. Creech," says my Lord, after acquainting me with that much of the letter, "thus by our persistence we have Mr. Ffooe where we want him. Her Majesty desires me to come to Windsor; 'twill yet be seen by all, that in this instance Crown and

Church were saved from as perilous a cabal as was ever conceived. . . ."

July 23, 1703

. . . my Lord, wishing to have the prisoner brought to Windsor so as to examine him in the presence of her Majesty and thus complete his triumph, once more caused a postponement of Mr. DeFoe's being pilloried. But he was gravely disappointed by the Chief Keeper at Newgate who apprised him that the prisoner could not be brought out of London, for it would be an escape and a discharge of his fine, and by law the prisoner could not be compelled afterwards to return to Newgate. This left my Lord a choice between himself braving the noisome circumstances of Newgate prison to hear Mr. DeFoe's confession or applying for a writ of *habeas corpus*. My Lord wrote to the Lord Keeper for such a writ; but meanwhile learned through the elder William Penn that Lord Privy Seal, the Duke of Buckinghamshire and Normanby, desired to be present at the prisoner's examination; and so, with a deep sigh and his eyes turned heavenwards, my Lord told me to prepare all for the visit to Newgate of himself and Lord Privy Seal.

The elimination of near a century's stench and filth being unfeasible, it was decided to have their lordships preceded by a dozen keepers who would brush the worst of the offal from their route and spray the air with sweet-smelling substances; others, armed with staves, were to repulse such prisoners as would try to petition their lordships by throwing themselves at their lordships' feet or accosting them in other ways; also, comfortable chairs were to be placed in Mr. DeFoe's cell and the cell to be whitewashed against crawling insects.

Such preparations did not remain unnoticed and increased the turbulence prevalent at Newgate to the point that some keeper said 'twas more like Bedlam; and a troop of constables was called in to aid in protecting their lordships. Despite all, some prisoners succeeded in breaking through—a big-breasted whore throwing her arms about the exquisite Lord Privy Seal and moistening his shoulder with her snot; there was great yowling and cursing as the keeper's staves cracked down on the prisoners' skulls, and blood flowed richly from noses and lips.

Through this uproar my Lord Nottingham moved with the greatest disdain, the torches playing their lights over his haggard features and making his eyes gleam strangely. Once he inquired if Mr. Ffooe was in his cell and, upon being assured by the Chief Keeper, continued on his way. Entering the cell, he greeted the prisoner civilly, saying, "I see, Mr. Ffooe, you've been writing; a more God-fearing piece, I hope, than your *Shortest Way*?"

"'Tis a long poem," says the prisoner, "a *Hymn to the Pillory*."

"Ah, good," says my Lord, "fear and contrition have since biblical times been the mainspring of some of the most excellent literature. But my Lord Privy Seal and I have not taken the pain of descending here for the purpose of discoursing on matters of art; rather, Mr. Ffooe, as you will have surmised, we wish to hear you finally divulge all you know pertaining to the writing and publication of *The Shortest Way with the Dissenters* and give an account of your accomplices and the full aims of this plot."

"I have surmised," says Mr. DeFoe, looking chagrined, "that your Lordships have come to rescind my sentence and to rescue me from this infernal hole, as was promised me if I pleaded guilty in court."

"A plea of guilty without a full confession is like a skin without wine," says my Lord. "And would you consent, Mr. Ffooe, to not wasting Lord Privy Seal's time and mine. You have clearly stated that you are prepared to make oath to me of all you know of the conspiracy, your accomplices et cetera."

"If it please your Lordship," says Mr. DeFoe, "when am I to have stated that, and to whom?"

"We have it on the authority of Mr. William Penn, the Quaker," says my Lord, "who informed several Lords of the Council thereof."

At this, Mr. DeFoe with flying fingers extracted from the papers on his table a scrawled sheet. "Here is the draft of my letter to Mr. William Penn, Sr., upon the visit to me of his son," says he. "With your Lordships' permission, I shall quote: *Sir, the proposal you are pleased to hint by your son from my Lord Nottingham of discovering parties is the same which his Lordship has often put upon me before. . . . I have answered his Lordship with the same assurance I did to the Privy Council: viz., that in the manner which they proposed it I really had no person to discover; that if my life were concerned in it I would not save it at the price of impeaching innocent men. . . . I solemnly affirm that other than what passes in conversation (and perhaps there is ill blood among people of my opinion more than enough), but other than that I have no accomplices, no set of men (as my Lord called them) with whom I used to concert matters of this nature, to whom I used to show or receive hints from them in reference to these matters; and therefore to put relief upon condition of such a nature is to offer me nothing at all. . . . But, Sir, my case is this: I came in upon the honour of the Government, being under bail that at least some of them consented to let me go away from, and pressed me to it. I agreed to give the court no trouble but to plead guilty to the indictment, even to all the adverbs, the seditiouslys, the maliciouslys, and a long rhapsody of the lawyers' et ceteras, and all this upon promises of being used tenderly. . . .*"

"'Tis enough now," says my Lord Nottingham, "we know the litany."

"If your Lordship please," says Lord Privy Seal, "you'll agree, Mr. Ffooe, that there's quite a contradiction between what Mr. William Penn, the Quaker, told several members of the Government and what you claim you wrote him. Did you tell William Penn, the son, when he saw you in your cell, substantially other than you wrote the father?"

"I did not," says Mr. DeFoe. "But 'tis impossible for me to vouch for what the younger Penn reported to the elder."

"When did you transmit your letter," says Lord Privy Seal, indolently eyeing the prisoner, "and by whom?"

"Oh, over a week ago," says Mr. DeFoe, "through the Chief Keeper of this gaol."

I was sent to summon the Chief Keeper, who admitted to having received the letter, but said that several days passed till his secretary could read it to him for his approval. By that time their lordships' visit was announced, entirely preoccupying him and his staff, so that the letter was posted only yesterday, and in view of the prisoner's strained circumstances, by carriers.

At this, Lord Privy Seal took a lace handkerchief from his sleeve and hid part of his face behind it; my Lord Nottingham however, who was exceedingly vexed, turned on the prisoner and in a frightening voice inquired, "Will you now speak, Mr. Ffooe? 'Tis the last time you are being asked. I have postponed your punishment and postponed it again; I will do so no more; when the stocks are closed about your neck 'twill be too late for regrets."

I saw Mr. DeFoe's shoulders sag as though they already carried the heavy crossbeam. "Cannot your Lordship understand," says he desperately, "that a man's free thought is not like the stick which the dog retrieves at a master's call? Or are you that steeped in the ways of orthodoxy that to your mind any idea not previously approved necessarily becomes part of a seditious plot?"

The blood rose to my Lord's face, colouring it livid. He wanted to speak but could not....

July 29, 1703

... constables and some soldiery having been placed in the side streets near Cornhill, I convinced myself that their captains were well instructed and then stationed some of the rogues hired for the occasion near the Royal Exchange at convenient distances from the pillory. Chief among them was Lemuel Finney, who had supplied himself with a bag of eggs, and stinking fish, and tomatoes, and rotten cabbages, a few paving stones among the lot for spice, and who assured me that missing one eye of his two not only did not dull the accuracy of his aim but actually sharpened it.

A half hour before the event, all sorts of folk began crowding the wide street so that within a brief time neither coaches nor other vehicles could pass through, and horse guards had to be brought up to open a lane for the cart on which Mr. DeFoe was being transported to the wooden scaffold at a few minutes before the noon hour. The prisoner stood on the cart, his hands free so he might support himself on the rails, and gazed with some apprehension over the mass of faces which were turned to him in sudden silence. He was heard by some to say to the driver, "Thank you for taking me *The Shortest Way*," after which he stepped from the cart on to the scaffold, the public hangman climbing up after him. The hangman quickly closed the stocks about the prisoner's neck and wrists so that his face, on which the sweat was gathering in large drops, was framed as on a picture and a paper was attached above his head reading: *Daniel Ffooe, for writing and publishing a seditious libel entitled, The Shortest Way with the Dissenters.*

The strange silence lasted while Mr. DeFoe tried to adjust himself to the discomfort of the crossbeam, putting as much of its weight as he could on the pole that supported it. Robin Hog, who had come to Cornhill despite his gout limped up to me. Wiping his forehead, "Mr. Creech," he whispers, "'tis likely you'll have trouble."

At this, a woman cried out and a cheer rose, "DeFoe!", and was joined by others shouting, "Ffooe!" and "DeFoe!" and "Halloo!" so that, with the echoes from the houses on either side of the street, the place resounded as though a giant-sized animal were broken loose and roaring its threat at us. The horses of the guard growing skittish, and the constables anxious, I thought it better to have the crowd forced away from the scaffold, but not so far as to impede the activity of my men planned for later. Meanwhile, I trusted that Mr. DeFoe would not have it all his way and that those present of the clergy or of other respectable calling would speak their mind. Instead, a number of women came upon the scene, most of them young and some of doubtful virtue, carrying nosegays and wreaths of flowers. The unsuspecting soldiers let them pass; whereupon the women proceeded to garland the scaffold among the huzzahs of the crowd and ribald jokes at the expense of Church and Judicature. At the same time, from taverns and chop houses near by, diverse people converged upon the pillory, raising tankards and bottles to toast the prisoner up high and cheer him for a brave fellow and a man of spirit, crying, "Keep it up, Mr. DeFoe!" and, "We're with you, Mr. Ffooe!" and, "The Shortest Way is the best way!"

So Robin Hog approached me once again. Leaning on his cane, "Mr. Creech," says he, "this has the earmarks of going against us; if ever you intend striking, 'tis now or never."

"Have patience, Mr. Stephens," says I, "it took us four and a half months to catch him, but we did; we'll give it a few minutes; the crowd's a fickle thing, and those who cried Hosannah will soon enough cry Crucify." And as at this moment Finney sneaked up and furtively winking inquired what I wished to have done, I told him to pass the word among his confederates to begin at the stroke of the half hour past noon with their shouting of invective and their pelting the prisoner.

Mr. DeFoe, this I could observe, was none too comfortable despite the various proofs of sympathy for him; the sun beat upon him, the sweat stung his eyes; flies and midges settled upon his face and hands without his being able to shoo them or scratch himself. Furthermore, he must be as aware as I was that the flowers and toasts were not the only salutations he might receive; he painfully twisted his head between the stocks and glanced about him as though trying to discern from where the next move would come.

As it was fairly quiet just then, I heard his groan; but at that moment the crowd broke and through it, from across the Exchange, rushed a horde of aproned boys, printers''prentices and the like, with baskets full of pamphlets and broadsheets, and started hawking at the top of their lungs, "The newest from the author of the *True-Born Englishman*!—*A Hymn to the Pillory*!, especially written and published for this day—and a new edition of *The Shortest Way*!—Buy them, read them, pass them on!" And while the constables and some of the soldiers were chasing the boys, these sold their wares on the run, and some, in preference to having the papers seized, scattered them over the crowd so they flew up like white birds, frightening the horses of the guards which neighed and reared and added to the general confusion; and high from a lantern post a young man with a bright, penetrating voice read out to the people,

"Hail! hieroglyphic State Machine,
Contrived to punish Fancy in!
Men, that are men, in thee can feel no pain;
And all thy insignificants disdain!"

At this, laughter broke loose, while the prisoner's lips trembled in a smile. The young man, perched too high for the reach of the constables, went on reading verse; but the general noise occasioned by the shouts of the soldiers continuing to hunt the boys, the clamour of spectators desiring to acquire the seditious wares, the screams of women being squeezed and shoved, the renewed cheers for the prisoner, left only snatches of the poem audible. In it, apparently, the author was listing those he thought should be in the pillory in his stead, *the Statesmen, who guide us with unsteady hand! the soldiers willing to be paid, and not to fight! the Colonels, who false masters bring! the coward Captains of the Fleet!*

The crowd howled for more, and the young man climbed higher on his post and declaimed,

"Jobbers and Brokers of the City Stocks . . .
That here they should remain
Till this enigma they explain:
How stocks should fall, when sales surmount the cost:
And rise again when ships are lost . . .
Some Churchmen next would grace thy Pews,
Who talk of Loyalty they never use . . .
Next bring some Lawyers to thy Bar!
These are the Mountebanks of State
Who, by the slight of tongue, can crimes create . . .
The Mastiffs of a Government
To Worry and run down the innocent! . ."

This was a close shot, and I looked for Robin Hog, who stood transfixed, as though a bolt had struck him. The young man, an actor by the quality of his voice, was once more heard through the din,

"But Justice is inverted when
Those Engines of the Law
Instead of pinching vicious men,
Keep honest ones in awe!"

'Twas too much; and I knew what my Lord Nottingham would have to say if it wasn't stopped. I gestured to the captain of the horse guards, and at the head of his men he rode as pretty an attack as you might wish to see, and from their horses' backs the guards took hold of the young man's legs and pried him loose from the lantern post, so that he landed on the pavement with a crack that set a resounding period to his last stanza.

Upon this, a hush settled over the crowd. A mere minute or two awaited the half-hour, and I thought I had it timed neatly, for Finney's missives would explode into the properly set mood; but now another voice rose—cracked, hoarse, strained, uncanny—and I realised it was the prisoner's,

"Tell us, Who 'tis, upon thy Ridge stands there,
So full of fault, and yet so void of fear?
And from the paper in his hat
Let all mankind be told for what! . . .
Tell them, it was because he was too bold!
And told those truths which should not have been told! . . .
Tell them, he stands exalted there
For speaking what we would not hear! . . .
To make men of their honesty afraid. . . ."

The voice seemed at the end of its strength, but it rallied and in a near-whisper, audible only to part of the crowd, spoke,

"Tell them, the men that placed him here,
Are scandals to the times!
Are at a loss to find his guilt,
And can't commit his crimes!"

The bell struck the half-hour. But nothing of what I had arranged for burst into the awful lull. I glanced about for Lemuel Finney and saw him, with his bag of missiles, making his way towards me. "Mr. Creech," says he, "'twould not work. We have as fine a band of cutthroats and villains as ever was gathered outside of Newgate, but they none of them would dare speak up against the humour of these people, or even throw the tail of a fish."

"So you start, Finney," says I, "if you please. It takes a good man to set an example, and you warranted that, being one-eyed, you aimed better than the others."

"Mr. Creech," says he, "I can hit the fly on a man's moustache without grazing his nose. But the fellow isn't born yet who could knock out a thousand people with one shot."

"Then give me your bag, Finney," says I. "At least I may use your ammunition."

He obliged gladly, and I found a paving stone that fit well to my hand, and raised my arm for the throw, shouting, "There's a rosebud for the great author . . ."

'Twas the last thing I knew, but for a loud thump on my skull and a shower of stars. . . .

August 3, 1703

. . . slowly opening my eyes I saw, as through a fog, the fat face and slovenly wig and snuff-bespattered collar of Robin Hog. The face grew larger, the mouth opened in concern, displaying a set of dirt-coloured but uncommonly large and capable teeth. "Why, Mr. Creech," says he, "seems you're creating a new fashion for perukes, all linsey-woolsey and tight about the head, and down to your brow and over your ears. A pretty picture, indeed, of a fine man and loyal servant of the Government, not much the worse for a crack on his cranium that would have laid a tenderer creature to eternal rest."

"Pray, Mr. Stephens," says I, "which date are you writing today?"

"The third day of August," says he, "a sunny day, not a cloud in the sky; 'tis an exceptional summer we're having."

I started counting in my mind and then asked him, "Have I been sleeping all this while, Mr. Stephens?"

"Sound as a babe, Mr. Creech," says he. "Not a move from you, or so much as a peep, since we took you home from the Exchange at Cornhill."

"Cornhill," says I, the events there returning piecemeal to memory, "I suppose Mr. DeFoe was duly dealt with in the end?"

"Duly dealt with?" says Robin Hog. "If it's duly that a mere writer of libels and doubtful rhyme triumphs over religion and established authority, 'twas duly. If it's duly that at the completion of his hour in the pillory he was hallooed down by the crowd and hailed their hero and symbol, 'twas duly. If it's duly that on the street you can't pronounce the simple syllable Foo without people telling you, there's a man's man, and what a scoundrelly

Government we're having, and maybe' tis time to think of another revolution, 'twas duly."

"But the other two times?" says I. "Don't tell me, Mr. Stephens, that the thing ended so scandalously in Cheapside, the following day, and at Temple Bar, the day thereafter? That Mr. DeFoe stood there in glory instead of shame? That he was king of the rabble instead of their butt, subversion and heresy thus being rewarded instead of given its deserts? Where were all the Queen's messengers and the force of the law? Where the agents secret and not so secret, the spies and informers and bullies and pimps on whom the state depends in its struggle against the ever-seditious mind, and on whom it lavishes its favours?"

"Ah, Mr. Creech," says he, with a sigh, "'twas as though with the loss of your valuable person the Government had lost its head. Lord Nottingham involved himself in an altercation with Lord Privy Seal and Lord Godolphin over the case; had they been deceived by Mr. DeFoe or not, and was her Majesty well served by the trial or not, and was it better to cancel two thirds of the judgement against Mr. DeFoe, and thus admit its injustice or permit him, by twice more placing himself in the pillory, twice more to pillory the established Church and Government, or had one best call in the military and let the soldiers bash the misled public's heads. And between arguing these and related matters, their Lordships took no decisive measures at all, and thus the affair took its deplorable course."

At which Mr. Robin Hog, his throat having dried up, began searching for a bottle of wine, a pitcher of beer, or anything potable; but finding nothing, his eye fell upon a letter on the sideboard that must have been delivered during my long unconsciousness. "Mr. Creech," says he, "I think I recognise the seal; 'tis from his Lordship."

Expecting the communication to contain a message of condolence at my misfortune, or cheer, or even praise, I begged Mr. Hog to break the seal and read the letter to me. Complying because of his gouty fingers with some difficulty, he then cleared his throat and read, "*Mr. Josiah Creech,* et cetera et cetera. *In view of your conspicuous failure in the matter of The Queen against DeFoe, the effect of which I trust I need not explain, it is deemed advisable that as of this date you separate from my office.* Signed, Nottingham."

"And that's all, Mr. Stephens?" says I.

"Mr. Creech," says he, "that's all."

A very good second man

A very good second man

"Robert!"

The man sitting below the fan turned languidly. Then he recognised me. "My God!" he jumped up, "where did you come from? And here, of all places! . . ." He pointed beyond the open porch at the dusty palm trees standing like battle-weary survivors of a lost battalion. A loudspeaker dangling from a whitewashed post was dinning into our ears a monotonous interchange of monotonous words first in our language, then in the language of this country.

"I came to cover the story," I said. "It's big news, our building this bridge for these people, especially big for back home. After all, our project was chosen over some of the fanciest Western competition. . . . Look at me telling you—the guy that built it. . . ."

"The guy that built it," said Robert, "is out there making a speech."

"Oh," I said.

"Whisky and soda?" Robert sat down and shoved bottles and a glass across the table. The fan, mounted under the ceiling, kept up a steady whir that gently stirred the thin strands of hair on his suntanned pate. He had got older. Thinner and older, with a stringy neck and tired, red-rimmed eyes. Maybe he was drinking too much.

"The guy that built it—who is he?" I asked.

"Fellow named Krivitsky," he said.

"I hope his engineering is better than his oratory," I said.

"You mean to tell me you never heard of Krivitsky?" Robert inquired. "What kind of journalist are you! He put the big viaduct across Lungfo Gorge, he built the causeway that links up Northern and Southern Machabar, he suspended the suspension bridge over the Blue Mvani. Don't you read the papers and the praise our great civil engineer has got and the credit he has brought to our Republic?"

He drank.

I remembered the press blurbs dimly, the newspapers and magazines: something about our Socialist Republic and those newly liberated countries being bridged by these bridges, and that we were exporting not just a structure and engineering know-how but friendship between nations. Except that I always thought. . . .

"I always thought Lungfo Gorge was your job, Robert!" I said. "Didn't you say so yourself, the last time we met?"

"That was four years ago," he said. "I've had to correct myself."

I gulped down my drink. My bush shirt, porous though it was, felt like a piece of medieval armour. The fan seemed to have trouble cutting through the thick, hot air. Krivitsky's voice boomed in on us, majestic, mellifluous.

"We used to call him the Mouse."

"Whom?" I asked, surprised at what looked like a switch of subject matter.

"Krivitsky," said Robert. "He has that sort of face, everything tapering towards the nose; but even the nose lacks character. And when he came in with his little mincing steps . . . No, he had no voice then at all. And everything he said, when he said anything, he prefaced with: Of course I may be wrong, I'm just the simple son of a simple workman. . . ."

"Robert," I said, "you're making it up. Or the heat is getting you down. . . ."

He laughed without mirth. "Go cover your story," he said. "Go gather those pearls of wisdom and spread them before the suffering public. I've heard Krivitsky's speech before. You have at least another fifteen minutes of it, with translation that makes thirty, enough to keep you busy and out of my hair."

I poured myself another drink, one third whisky, two thirds soda, and settled in the chair. Down there, they have those chairs with the long arm rests; you stretch your feet on the extended arm rests; with a drink at your side it's the only comfortable position in that country, nine months out of twelve.

"Go ahead, Robert," I said. "I *am* covering the story."

He looked at me across the rim of his glass. "You are? . . . They won't print it. It's not pretty. It lacks a positive perspective and doesn't spur you to perform heroic feats of Socialist labour."

"You engineer steel and I engineer souls," I said. "So don't you worry about my branch of engineering. I'll find the positive perspective."

"All right," he said, rubbing his eyes and unbuttoning his shirt, "it all began with the mix-up at Lungfo Gorge. Somebody back home in the cadre department decided that Krivitsky should come along to Lungfo Gorge. Maybe somebody wanted to get rid of him for a while, or had a bad conscience because the simple workman's simple son never got anywhere, or maybe. . . ."

"But you, too, are the simple son of a simple workman!"

"I started out as a welder," said Robert impatiently. "Should I advertise it?"

I chased away some tired flies that had come to rest on my ankle. I knew the road Robert had travelled, his days full of back-breaking work, the nights given to study, and all this interspersed with the years in jail while Hitler lorded it over Europe. . . .

"I neither liked nor disliked the man," he went on. "If I had any feeling about him it was a sort of pity—a mousy creature trying to be somebody, knowing he was of no earthly use for the job and yet compelled always to give an opinion, speaking neither Russian nor English nor any of the Asiatic tongues, and really quite lost. . . . Whenever I found an off-minute I translated for him or showed him the sights or tried to give him a notion of the country he was in and its people, until he told me that, as a Marxist, he didn't need to see much of any country to know what was the matter with it. Even after that I included him whenever we dealt with the local engineers or the authorities or the people and their organisations. You know how it is, you know how people in these parts are when it comes to judging Europeans, even from Socialist Europe—and here we were just two guys from our Republic. I didn't want to have it said that out of two men sent to help them, one was a dud."

He paused. The voice over the loudspeaker, which had furnished the static to his story, grew distinct. It was talking about our Socialist Republic and this newly liberated country being bridged by this bridge, and that we were exporting not just a structure and engineering know-how but friendship between nations. . . .

"When the Lungfo Gorge project was finished," Robert's eyes closed, "they had a little ceremony—the usual thing, speeches, flags, a toast or two, the cutting of a ribbon before the first train rumbled across with the bunting flying and people hanging from its engine like grapes. Ah, it was beautiful, the engine with the red star at its bow. It was beautiful because it was the first engine ever to cross the gorge, high up, like one of those tiny bugs on a leaf of grass that you see on Chinese water colours, and it was opening up a new land for I don't know how many millions of people. . . ."

The neck of the bottle clanked hard against his glass; his hand shook in the pouring.

"Easy," I said. "Take it easy."

"It gets you, sometimes," he said, leaving open what it was that got him.

"Can't we shut off that noise?" I inquired.

He shrugged, and went on, "I had to make the speech then. I

tried to express something of what I felt. I'm not much good at it. I see a thing, I sense it down to my finger tips but there's a block before I can get it into the right words. That time, though, the block melted away. I thought of all the people who had worked together, the thousands of peasants who had shovelled and picked and carted and carried, the workers who had hung above the dizzying depth, riveting and welding, through icy storms, through desert heat, through nights when you wouldn't chase a dog out. I guess I must have said it the right way, because afterwards some of those peasants and some of those workers came and hugged me as if I was their brother. And then, a few days later, somebody shows me an item in the newspaper of the nearest district town and translates for me that the world-famous civil engineer B. R. Krivitsky, sent to us by the working people of our Socialist Brother Republic and so forth and so on, on the occasion of the opening of Lungfo Gorge Bridge towards the construction of which he so richly contributed and so forth and so on, spoke in the most moving words and said and so forth and so on."

I laughed.

"I laughed, too," said Robert. "What difference does it make, I thought. Some local newsman who didn't know either of us from a hole in the wall had inquired in the construction office and had got our names mixed up, and so Krivitsky had finally broken into the press, even though it was printed in letters he couldn't decipher and in a town that wasn't much more than a collection of mud huts. In fact I gave a copy of the paper to him as a souvenir, and he pocketed it with lots of thanks."

"Didn't he see the joke?"

Robert thought for a moment. "Maybe," he finally said. "But if so, on whom was the joke? At any rate, I don't think he has a sense of humour. If he had, none of what followed could have happened."

"*What* followed?"

"That damned news item kept dogging us all the way from Lungfo Gorge to the home office. As we reached the capital of the country, the story reached it, and greeted me from the front page of the English language paper they publish there. At Moscow airport we changed planes. I just had time to buy the evening paper—second page, third column: Record length bridge built in record time at record height inaugurated by the famous civil engineer B. R. Krivitsky. And by the time our plane sets down on the soil of our little Republic, the photographers are waiting for Krivitsky and the newsreel people shoot a smart item of Krivitsky coming down the gangway and being greeted by six pioneer girls with a bouquet of pink roses. Maybe you saw it at your local cinema."

I got up. As soon as I left the reach of the fan, the heat enveloped me in its merciless shroud. But I moved on, out of the room, across the porch, out of the shade, up to that whitewashed post. With a flick of my thumb I unsheathed the big blade of my pocketknife and cut the cable.

Into the blessed quiet sounded the laughter from the back where Robert sat. I returned to him. I re-parked my legs on the arm rests of my chair and stopped his laughter with an angry motion of my hand and asked, "And what about him? What did he say?"

"Oh, him! He protested, with exactly the right amount of modesty: it was too much of an honour for him, and I must accept half of his roses, and the news photographers must take at least one shot of the two of us, him and me, surrounded by the six little pioneer girls. . . ."

"Touching," I said.

"Touching," Robert confirmed.

"But in your home office they surely knew," I said. "They surely knew who had been sent and the capabilities of each of you!"

"God, yes," he said. "Sure they knew. But the funny thing about people is that most of them don't quite trust their own judgement. I saw it from the way they questioned me in the cadre department. They never put it in so many words, but I could smell it. Maybe there was something to the story that had come from Lungfo Gorge and had been printed in the most important newspapers of our Republic. Maybe at some point or other I had fallen down on my job or lost control of things or simply got ill, and Krivitsky had taken over. That's why he'd been sent there, after all, to take over in case of an emergency, hadn't he? And could you entirely disregard a report printed in our most important papers? Someone from the Ministry had already phoned and hinted that in view of the importance of the Lungo Gorge project for the friendship between our Republic and the brotherly people of other Socialist countries as well as with the newly liberated people of the underdeveloped nations, engineer Krivitsky ought to be in line for honorable mention, a premium, and a medal at the occasion of the next official holiday."

"No!" I said.

"No," he said, "he didn't get it. Not that time."

The flies had come back. The flies, in that part of the world, seemed to move in tribes, and where the chief heads they head, and where he sits down, they all sit, braving whatever you try to do to them. The flies were again on my ankle.

"You've got to pickle them," he said. "Try whisky."

I took the bottle, filled my glass, and hit the flies with my notebook. "I'd rather pickle myself," I said. The cover of my notebook was pimpled with dead flies. The chief of the flies took his tribe to the lampshade for regrouping.

"Why didn't you speak up," I said, "like a man?"

"Why didn't I?" Robert frowned. "I guess it would have been too awkward."

"Awkward, hell! The time for feeling awkward and having other noble sentiments will come; we're working on it; but it will take a few years."

"All right," he said, "put yourself in my spot. Here I am, the big guy, with an established reputation, with so many big jobs behind me, raising a fuss about what amounts to a typographical error. And there is Krivitsky, the Mouse, the simple son of a simple workman, and it's his first chance to prove himself on a job, and I squelch him. I say he did nothing at Lungfo Gorge, I did everything, including the final speech. What's it going to sound like? Good or bad?"

"Bad," I said.

"All right," he went on, "they've always overlooked him because he's so little and mousy and inhibited. But others, they worry, have not overlooked him—some newsman far away at Lungfo Gorge, a score or two newspaper editors, and now even someone from the Ministry. Maybe they've made a mistake? They're uncertain. Their conscience bothers them. One word against him from me, and they'll discover they've always known that Krivitsky is the Republic's greatest engineer and that it's guys like me who have conspired to keep him down."

"I see," I said.

"Sure you see," said Robert. He drank, wiped his mouth and then his forehead with the back of his hand and flicked off the moisture. "Sure you see . . . and he saw it too. He played it shrewdly. He curbed himself, though his new personality was beginning to burst through the seams. He still minced about and prefaced his commonplace remarks in his usual manner, but his remarks became more frequent and their tone more authoritative, and at our office conferences he sometimes sat grandly with his arm hooked over the back rest of his chair."

Robert draped himself over his chair, his twisted posture conjuring up a perfect blend of conceit and false modesty. A second later he was swatting at the flies which had descended on his sweating neck, and the disgusting image was gone.

"Then came the Machabar Causeway," he said, "and the problem of who was to go and be in charge of its construction. Ever driven over that causeway?"

I shook my head. "But I read that it was a hell of a difficult job."

"It wasn't easy," he said. The flies had moved off, and he was relaxed again, nursing his drink. "Not that the Bay of Machabar is so deep, but it practically has no bottom. Whatever you pour in is sucked up by the silt—uncanny—and part of the causeway had to be a bridge that could be pivoted to let the ships by."

"They sent you?"

He nodded.

"With Krivitsky?"

He nodded again.

"And you took that?"

He drank. He tried to refill his glass, but the bottle was empty and he chucked it out. It thudded on to the porch and clattered down the stairs.

"We'd better stop drinking, anyhow," I said.

"You don't understand," he said. "You don't understand at all what this is about. There were maybe half a dozen men in the whole world who could have built that causeway, and of them only one resided in our Republic. . . ."

"So you could have dictated your terms!" I threw in.

He waved me off. "They called me in for a little talk with the head of the cadre department," he said, "in the presence of a couple of other big shots. They congratulated me on the big job they were handing me and told me what a challenge it was and how important it was politically and that they felt sure I would acquit myself as I always had, and that they were awfully happy to be able to send out the same team which had worked so harmoniously at Lungfo Gorge . . . I stopped them at that point."

He paused. He chuckled. His eyes groped for the whisky, found none, grew angry.

"But why? they asked me. What was my objection to Krivitsky? The man had nothing but praise for me; he went around telling everybody what a great engineer I was and how I inspired the workers and how he was sure that without me they'd still be trying to bridge Lungfo Gorge and wasn't I being subjective about the unfortunate mistake of a distant newspaper reporter. . . ."

He noticed my grin.

"Don't worry!" he said. "I told them! I told them to let Krivitsky build pissoirs, but that he was no good for that causeway. I told them to send him to the North Pole, but not to Machabar Bay. I told them. . . ."

"And they?"

"They smiled. They patted me on the back. Why did I want to be so stubborn, they said. Did I really want to place myself and my own judgement above that of the collective? The collective felt that Krivitsky was not the very best in the field, you had to take into account that he was only the simple son of a simple workman and, looked at objectively, it was really my duty to help him develop himself. . . ."

He broke off. "I'm dry from all that talk," he said. "I must have another drink."

"Drink lemonade," I said. "Or tea."

He shook himself. "You know," he said, "after they've badgered you for a while, you begin to get soft. You begin to think that maybe you didn't look at things quite as they are, and isn't it possible that you're mistaken, and you mustn't let your personal likes and dislikes run away with you, and there are greater things at stake than Krivitsky's coming to Machabar Bay or not . . . But I insisted that it be made absolutely and a hundred per cent clear who was the chief; and they said of course, and if that was my worry I should forget it. . . ."

He got up. He folded last week's paper into a swatter and began hitting at the flies, wildly, unsystematically, but with great effect. Finally, breathless, he fell back on to his chair.

"When we arrived at Machabar Bay," he said, "I found out that both of us had been given exactly equal status."

"You should have expected that," I said. "I'm a firm believer in collective action and collective thinking, but when anyone uses the collective as a club over your head, there's usually something fishy at hand. Why didn't you turn around, then and there? Why didn't you fly home and tell them to let Krivitsky build the causeway?"

"Are you kidding?" he said. "I'm an engineer!"

"I understand," I said. I looked at him, his stringy neck, his tired eyes, his sunken cheeks, and I remembered him as I had seen him years back, straight and strapping, and I knew that he had left some of himself in the steel girders vibrating across Lungfo Gorge, and in the concrete of Machabar Causeway, and in the cables that held the bridge over the Blue Mvani, and in everything he had helped to build so as to make the world a better place to live in. "I understand," I said again.

"I didn't have much time to worry over Krivitsky at Machabar Bay," he resumed. "I was as busy as a one-armed paperhanger. I had a new problem to solve every hour on the hour as the causeway grew and, with it, the people who worked on it. I just noticed Krivitsky occasionally. He had organised a motor launch for himself and he had found a broken-down, rum-sodden type to serve as translator, and he appeared in his launch wherever he saw men at work and observed them, arms akimbo, giving a significant nod or two to his swaying adjutant. Sometimes people would put a question through this character and Krivitsky would furnish one of those cryptic answers that became even more cryptic in translation. It was very impressive and the administrative personnel began to look up to him. A man who had nothing to do but drive around in a launch and watch other people work must be a real boss. The local officials began to address themselves to him, and he started inviting them for round trips over the project and explaining to them the progress of the work according to his limited lights and the limited capabilities of his translator. One day he was overheard telling a beturbaned and bejewelled guest who had noticed me and inquired about me: Ah, yes, him! . . . he's also an engineer . . . a very good second man. . . . I got the story days later, and somehow I didn't get around to confronting Krivitsky with it, and then the man who related it to me had gone, so everything became hearsay and nebulous, and suppose Krivitsky denied it or blamed his drunken translator?"

"After the causeway was finished," I asked, "who spoke?"

Robert lowered his head. "We both did." If ever there had been a moment when he felt ashamed of himself, this must have been it. "I spoke at the beginning, and he at the end of the ceremony."

I reached into the back pocket of my trousers and placed before him the hip flask I carry for emergencies.

"Thanks," he said.

"You're welcome," I said. And after a moment, "You said, you both spoke. And in the papers back home, I suppose, his name was mentioned and yours not. Right?"

"Right."

"And then what happened?"

"Nothing. We got home, and the Blue Mvani project was already waiting for us."

"Us?"

Robert uncorked my flask. "They were quite blunt, this time. They said Krivitsky had proved that he deserved an opportunity. They had received a great number of reports from the local authorities at Machabar Bay, all of them unanimous in their praise of Krivitsky's work. They were going to let Krivitsky head the Blue Mvani job, and they wanted me to go along to do the detail work while Krivitsky would devote himself to the overall directing of the project, so to speak."

"Pretty raw," I said.

He sniffed at my flask. The smell seemed to satisfy him. "Damn it," he said, "if that remark of Krivitsky's didn't flash back into my mind, then, and I asked them, you mean to say I'm a very good second man."

I laughed.

"They looked at one another," he said, "and then they looked at Krivitsky, and then they said, well, that's what it amounted to. At that moment Krivitsky unhooked himself from the back rest of his chair and minced over to me and said he wouldn't hear of any such thing. There was no first man and no second man, there was only the collective, and either we went together to the Blue Mvani, or he wouldn't go either. It was a marvellous show."

"He must have been scared stiff," I said, "of that Blue Mvani."

"A marvellous show!" repeated Robert. He poured some of the stuff in my flask into his glass and listened to its blub-blub. "The head of the cadre department came round the desk and took my hand and put it in Krivitsky's hand and told us to shake and pointed out to me how much more generous Krivitsky's attitude was than mine had been before we left on the Machabar Causeway job, and that Krivitsky had shown us all a practical application of our new ethics, and that every one of us should learn from it."

"Why didn't you quit?" I said.

Robert drank. He drank my whisky straight, without bothering about the soda. "Because I knew the importance of the Blue Mvani project," he said, "for that country and for ours. And because I'm a responsible citizen," he added, "of a Socialist Republic."

He fell silent. The chief of the flies had decided to withdraw his tribe, and the only things moving were the fan and the lightly swaying crowns of the palms. Then there were voices, one of them in our language. The inauguration ceremony seemed to be over.

People, some dark-faced, some of lighter complexion, were saying noisy good-byes outside. Only one man stepped forward. He minced up the stairs, on to the porch, and into the room. As he saw me, he hesitated.

"This," said Robert, "is engineer Krivitsky." And pointing at me, he explained to Krivitsky that I had come to cover the opening of the new bridge and the inauguration ceremonies.

"I didn't see you out there," Krivitsky said to me, with a slight undertone of suspicion and a guarded glance at Robert.

"A good newspaperman," I replied, "can get his story anywhere." I looked at him. The people who had dubbed him the Mouse hadn't been wrong, but he had become a fat mouse, bloated with the grain of success and the bacon of self-complacency. "So you built this bridge, Mr. Krivitsky?" I inquired, indifferently.

Again Krivitsky glanced at Robert. His uncertainty was blatant.

"Well, you're the chief civil engineer," I prodded, "aren't you?"

"I am, yes. . . ."

"So you built the bridge!"

"I did," he said, "in a manner of speaking . . . You know . . . there are always the workers . . . I'm a simple workman's son myself. . . ."

"So if it was you who built the bridge," I asked, "do you think it will stand?"

"Stand?" Krivitsky's face contracted around his nose and seemed to shrivel into something scared and ugly. "Stand?" he said, puzzled and outraged, "what do you mean?"

"Well . . ." I turned to Robert, "what do *you* think? Will it stand?"

Robert raised his glass. A finger's width of my whisky was left in it. A slow smile spread over the lines on his face.

"How can the bridge stand," I persisted, "if *he* built it?"

"Don't worry!" said Robert. "That bridge will stand!" He drank and then smashed the glass against the doorpost as if christening it in place of the bridge. He looked at Krivitsky who had ducked. He laughed. "This bridge will stand," he said, "because people built it, our people back home, and people here . . . and because I am a very good second man . . ." his voice rose, "and because I happen to be a Communist!"

Across the fence

Across the fence

He moved here the summer that Tonda and I broke up; the two events, though quite unconnected, form part of the same pattern in my mind.

He arrived with a whole troop. They came in three black limousines and spread over the ground as though they were combing it for rabbits. Except for him, they all looked alike—youngish men, with thick necks and heavy jowls and narrow-set, pale eyes. He was lean, with a face that seemed to have gone through a hardening process; he had the brows and forehead of an intellectual, but his hands were too big and dangled as though from disuse and unaccustomed to it. He moved with a marked casualness, but I noticed that from under his reddened, swollen lids he was studying me.

I'm not beautiful. The spark I once had and which made up for whatever else I didn't have was choked by the four children I have borne and by the years with Tonda. Nor am I what they call interesting. I can sit through a whole evening with everybody laughing and chatting and never say a word; people forget I'm there, and if I become thirsty I have to serve myself.

Perhaps he wanted to inquire how the soil was, or about traffic on week-ends or how long it had taken us to clear the bulrushes from our section of the beach. When you come to a new place you want to know such things; and it was only ten days since the building inspector of the township had surveyed the plot next to ours and the abandoned shack on it, and then the truckloads of building materials had begun to arrive.

Finally, to break the weight of his gaze, I said, "The strawberries . . . they're big this year . . . juicy. . . ."

"Are they?" There was a hedge between us that had grown wild with brambles. He came closer, his eyes still grilling me.

I felt then, as I often felt later in his encounters with Tonda or with guests of ours, that he watched you for that quick move that meant danger. Not far from him a couple of the thick-necked people were observing us, adding to the impression. I picked a handful of berries and held them out to him, across the hedge, as proof of my claim.

"Oh, thank you." He was startled. "They give me hives." He was about to turn. "You're Mrs. Ondrákova, aren't you?"

"Yes."

"I'm Pavel B. . . ." He gave a name that everyone knew, though press, radio, and television rarely mentioned it. "We shall be neighbours, Mrs Ondrákova. Anna Ondrákova, is it?"

"Anna."

He smiled, briefly.

I began to feel apprehensive at his moving on to that empty lot which stretched, a long, narrow patch of weeds, down to the lake. Why didn't a man of his status build his summer cottage where the others like him had theirs? Here he would be an outsider, a blight that stilled the laughter and the voices.

"Of course I shall have a fence built," he said. "I think you'll prefer that too. You wouldn't want your children to stray. . . ."

"Don't you like children?"

His heavy lids rose. "I like children. I like dogs, too." And after a pause, "I like people."

Tonda didn't commit himself about the new neighbour. Whenever Tonda came out from town, which was seldom enough, he observed the progress that had been made next door and remarked on it—not enviously and not with that slight sneer usual to him, rather with the detachment he saved for comments on some phenomenon in his laboratory.

Even though the progress was astonishing. In a time when the acquisition of a sack of cement required complicated deals involving cartons of American cigarettes, the neighbouring plot teemed with workmen who had an ample supply of steel, concrete, tiles, woods, glass, lead, copper, up-to-date machinery, cases of beer. They erected in a matter of days a white, red-roofed bungalow with picture windows overlooking the lake, with a flagstone terrace, a two-car garage and, discreetly off to the side, a smaller bungalow to house the thick-necked young men. Other workers tackled the years' growth of weeds, turned up the soil, enriched and fattened it till it steamed with fertility, terraced it, seeded it, and planted it, while down at the lake the bulrushes fell in sheaves, and yellow sand was spread by the truckload.

The brambled hedge remained; it grew on our land. But beyond it the fence was set up. It wasn't one of those fences you see elsewhere, repulsive, forbidding, with concrete posts linked by wire mesh and crowned with stands of steel thorns; this fence of field stone and gnarled roots artificially aged and joined by a weave of willow and hawthorn fitted itself into the landscape; it was no more than shoulder-high but difficult to climb.

The fence especially aroused Tonda's admiration. It showed, he said at dinner, not just thoughtfulness but an aristocratic bent—Tonda had been an exile in England during the war and knew the impenetrable, carefully groomed hedges that kept curious eyes from seeing manor house and grounds.

"Tonda," I said, "they did away with the aristocracy in ths country."

"Of course." A sneer tinged his smile. "I spoke of a state of mind which, if I know my Marx, is determined by a man's circumstances. Shouldn't we ask him over?"

I would no more have thought of inviting the President. But I could see Tonda's point. Long ago, Tonda should have been named head of the institute; but he had been in England during the war, and for reasons defying logic this counted against him in his cadre file. A word from Pavel B., and the objections might be dropped.

"I think it would be awkward," I said, "and most likely he would refuse."

"Not if *you* asked him," he said complacently. "You could make an effort at a chance meeting—across that fence, for instance. . . ."

"I *have* met him," I said, "when there was only the hedge."

"Oh." He looked at me as if he had just noticed me.

"It's your institute, Tonda. Do your own waiting at the fence."

"You know, dear, that I can't come out here more frequently."

"I know. I have to stay in the country so you and Miss Blahova won't feel inhibited in our flat in town."

"I wasn't thinking of the institute. Not primarily. I was thinking of the children, their future."

"And that's my department?"

"Ours, dear. Ours." He shrugged. "As you like. When it comes to proprieties, I've always put your judgement above mine."

Soon I knew more about the personal side of Pavel B.'s life—his habits, his routine—than anyone outside his immediate entourage, and I doubt if they knew as much. Children are always sharp-eyed and curious, especially in their early teens, and my three boys took the presence of the thick-necked men as a challenge.

They knew when B. arrived and with how many people, and how many stayed for dinner and how many overnight. They had names for some of his regular visitors, based on personal characteristics: Curley, and Crosseye, and Pegleg, and the Boxer, and the Weasel, and one whom they called Comrade Houndtooth. I was worried that someone would overhear the boys or that Tina, in her irrepressible five-year-old soprano, would prattle in the village store or on the street. Women visitors at Pavel B.'s bungalow were few; but when any arrived, I was immediately informed. The women stayed two and a half hours, three at most; they were driven off in one of the black limousines. Apparently it was a different woman each time; or the boys didn't get a good enough look at them to type them. In warm weather, one or the other of them would take a dip in the lake before retiring into the bungalow; there was never the same bathing suit, never the same figure, that I can attest to.

In the beginning I felt discomfort, if not fear, at prying into B.'s affairs. I never discovered the boys' observation posts or how many they had; I had my own. Nature, leaving a narrow gap in the hedge, and the workmen, leaving a sort of niche in the fence, had collaborated in creating it; the field stones formed a seat, a red beech overhead afforded shade and camouflage; I sat there for the quiet and seclusion of the spot, even on days when B. was not in the country. From my seat, the whole view unfolded—the red-roofed bungalow, the terraced gardens slanting to the golden beach, and the greenish lake. B. liked to swim. He had powerful arms to match his huge hands; they cut the water as though they were punishing it for some crime he could not otherwise prosecute. He liked to stand on his terrace and gaze at points distant: a monument to himself. He liked to walk the serpentine path that led him from terrace to terrace, slowly, very erect, the fingers hooked behind the small of his back. At one point, the path brought him quite close to me; I held my breath as he seemed to stare at me, or through me or behind me; and I could well understand the fear this man inspired.

That Saturday, Tonda came out. Miss Blahova's mother, I later learned, had suffered a stroke, and Miss Blahova had taken a train to the village in Moravia where the old woman lay dying—which left Tonda with time on his hands. He sat about, drank moodily and was glad when Pospishil, the writer, arrived to join him in killing the bottle. They soon talked of B. Pospishil, who knew God and the world, was full of stories and he told them with relish—B. and the President; B. holding forth at an international jurists' congress; B. at the trials.

"Of course," said Pospishil, twirling his glass, "in his capacity B. had to be present at the executions—at least the important ones. Jan Vejner's was big enough, and B. knew Vejner personally—they had worked in the same ministry, and on the same newspaper, and in the same department of the Central Committee. Jan Vejner was hung at dawn on a Monday. As he walked towards the gallows, he suddenly stopped and said to B., "This week starts great, doesn't it?" B. didn't even blink as he answered, "For you, certainly."

"I would like to correct you."

I froze. Pospishil turned white; Tonda jumped up and began to stammer.

"As a matter of fact Jan Vejner didn't say anything." B. stood in the door, a dark figure against the last light of day. "He couldn't speak. Nor was he walking; two guards had to half carry, half drag him to where he died." He probably saw the horror on my face. "I had the doctor give him a shot the night before, Mrs Ondrákova. I thought it best to blank his mind."

"Won't you—won't you sit down," said Tonda.

B. stepped into the room. He kissed my hand and apologised, "I knocked at the door. I thought I heard someone say, 'Come in'." And turning to Tonda, "Having met your charming wife, I was eager to meet you as well, Professor Ondrák. A neighbour is a neighbour; one never can tell when one needs a neighbour's help. . . ."

He sat down and, accepting the glass that Tonda hastily had filled for him, said to Pospishil, "You literary men will twist everything for the sake of a good line. That's what makes you such a hazard."

. . . . .

I thought then that I detected an uncertainty in him. With his alertness to Tonda and, obviously, to Pospishil, went a guardedness against some enemy at his back—perhaps the thick-necked young men. Had he escaped their protection for the evening? Or were they watching from the distance and by means of electronic devices listening in to what was being said? Were the members of that restricted group to which B. belonged prisoners as much as rulers; was their power over life and death a rope around their necks as much as a whipcord?

The question pursued me. But aside from that, the evening gave me a lift. I had a man who paid attention to me, addressed me repeatedly, even offered to help set the table. Tonda's sneer turned into grudging co-operation; for the first time in ages Tonda cut bread, carried a tray, fetched the mineral water—despite Pospishil's silly, alcoholic jibes. B. seemed to relish the situation and salted it by remarks on how young I looked, and that I had a generous mouth and that my white-trimmed hostess apron was perfect for my figure. I kept blushing like a 16–year-old, but I held on to my wits and brought up Tonda's institute when I thought the moment favourable. B. responded, yes, he had heard of the research done there, and one of his reasons for dropping by was that he wanted a personal impression of Professor Ondrák because, confidentially, there had been discussions on a reorganisation of some of the academy's institutes.

Tonda was weighing B.'s words. As the French cognac in the bottle diminished, his eyes grew cool and his lips thinned out. His answers to B.'s queries, scientific, political, psychological, became monosyllabic; and he snarled at Pospishil, who was gurgling happily over his drink and hiccuping, "The week's—starting great —it sure—is!"

When, finally, B. had gone and Pospishil had passed out on his bed in the attic room, Tonda turned on me.

"But you told me I was to . . ." I tried to defend myself.

He cut me off.

"Your institute, you told me," I insisted, "the children . . ."

He held his head as though despairing of my ever learning the simplest things in life.

"You think B.'s so big that I have to crawl up his anus?"

"Isn't he?"

"That he just drops in for a chat with some physics professor and a flirt with the professor's wife—doesn't that indicate something to you? A man who is secure in his power doesn't need to make himself popular."

"Perhaps he's just neighbourly. He once told me he likes people."

"He does, does he? . . . He has signed more death warrants than he cares to remember; he has broken men till they were gibbering idiots who would admit to anything; he has bought people, coerced people, tortured people—but *liked* them?"

"That's Pospishil's line on him. Pospishil is destructive. Besides, you have no right to throw stones, Tonda. You were ready to have me stand at that fence and make eyes at him as long as you thought he might hand you your institute—regardless of whether he was a gangster or a saint."

"And to you he's a saint."

"Well, at least he is considerate and courteous."

"You get along with him; I noticed that." He smiled. "I've always seen you as some gangling, helpless female who couldn't be left to fend for herself. I gladly correct that opinion."

"That means, you and Miss Blahova. . . ."

"At this stage of my life, Anna, my aim isn't to change horse collars. But that doesn't concern you."

"No, it doesn't," I said.

There was much dickering on the custody of the children, on financial matters, on the flat in town, and on the cottage. The proceedings dragged; I lost count of how many stamps were needed on how many documents to rend asunder what God had so injudiciously joined. Not that I lost all sight of Pavel B.—I heard his limousine and the cars of his entourage drive up; once or twice I saw him gaze from his terrace towards the far shore of the lake. But my fence seat remained unused, and whenever I thought of it I feared the lush growth of that summer might have covered it over.

Nor did Tonda's anticipation of B.'s decline seem correct. At least I saw no diminishing of Pavel B.'s power. His name, when mentioned at all, was coupled with every title due him; his guards, if anything, increased in number.

Finally the divorce decree was handed down. Custody of the children was given to me. Tonda kept the flat in town; I got the cottage. Tonda was to pay for the children's upkeep, a minimum, and nothing for me. Why shouldn't women, having equal rights, work when they were capable? I had two hands like the next woman.

I found the seat in the fence. After clearing away branches and leaves and moss and cobwebs, I settled myself in it, still too numb to think of what I really expected or if I expected anything. B.'s terraced garden had burst out in the blues and pinks and yellows of the gardeners' colour design; the light sparkled in the gentle spray from the irrigation pipes and broke, at certain angles, into a rainbow.

Whether my presence was reported to him, whether he had noticed or sensed it—B. descended the serpentine path, hands linked behind his back, his shirt open at the throat. For a moment it appeared as though he would again look through me or beyond me and pass by, but he stopped and unsmilingly said, "You know, my men disapprove of your sitting here."

I got up.

"Stay. I told them you may stay. I told them you had a poetic nature and liked to sit here and dream."

"And they believed you?"

"Well . . . On the other hand, you've been checked and cleared."

As we faced one another across the fence, my having been checked and cleared seemed less important to me than his knowledge that this niche, this waiting, this calm held meaning for me. With all that must have been preying on his mind at the time, this man had given thought to me.

"We can't stand here for ever," he said. "We're being watched."

But he made no move to leave.

"Good-bye, then," I said.

His hand that had dangled awkwardly rose in brief protest. "I owe you an invitation, Mrs. Ondrákova. Why don't you come over now, for a cup of coffee and a view of my garden, from my angle?"

His face had remained unrelenting; his voice was almost gruff. I hesitated.

"You did want some help, didn't you?" he said. "It couldn't be a long visit, at any rate. I expect people for a conference."

I watched him retracing his steps up the serpentine. At its turn, the evening light accented his white, short-cropped hair above his lean face, giving him an ascetic, almost monkish look. I could imagine him as an inquisitor presiding over the torture of a heretic, suffering along with his victim and pleading for a confession so the sinner could partake in the joys of heaven after having been cleansed in the flames of the stake.

The interior of his bungalow, though, was anything but ascetic. B. was the perfect host, at ease among the gleaming copper of his kitchenette, effortlessly producing little delicacies and setting them before me with a grace that I would never have believed his heavy hands capable of. "I've been a widower for years," he explained, "and, as you see, I enjoy my independence."

He urged me to eat and seemed to be pleased at my sampling his stuffed olives, his sturgeon in aspic, his cold *rôti de veau*, his soufflé. He drank almost nothing, apologising that he must keep a clear head for the conference, but poured one Scotch after the other for me and insisted that I drink them. His eyes kept travelling over me, and he said, "You look as though you could stand being spoiled, Mrs Ondrákova. Anna. I may call you Anna?"

I tried to laugh. "And why would *you* want to spoil me?"

He leaned forward, his hands pushing aside dishes and glassware and gripping the edge of the narrow table on my side. "Because you're a human being."

That gave a pretty wide range to his charity, I thought.

"A rare commodity, Anna—a human being. Don't you ever study faces and see them for what they are—gargoyles—don't you ever feel surrounded, don't you—"

He broke off, leaned back. "I'm sorry, Anna. Did I frighten you?"

"I'm not afraid of you," I said.

"That, too, is rare." He relaxed. "But we wanted to discuss what could be done for you. Four children . . ." He shook his head. "That ex-husband of yours . . . Those courts . . ."

It turned out he had followed the case but had chosen not to interfere.

"People believe that power is something absolute." He frowned. "Now this B., they'll say, he can do anything he pleases. Actually, my hands are tied by more strings than yours; whatever I do, say, decide, is affected by so many divergent forces that sometimes it makes me wonder that anything gets done."

He moved his fingers and scrutinised his hands as if he were tracing the strings that tied them.

"And one gets tired of shoving figures about on a chessboard that never empties. That's a mistake, of course—getting tired. In this game you can't afford it. They sense it. They've got a nose for it. Their sense of smell is keener than any wolf's. You sweat. They smell the sweat and they know: this one's weakening. And then comes this imperceptible withdrawal, this tiny gap between you and the pack, this first gleam in their eyes—and you know that, next thing, there'll be the growl and the baring of fangs. . . ."

He turned and gazed at the Napoleonic clock on the mantelpiece. He realised that he had told too much, and he tried wiping it off the board with a sudden cold smile.

"Excuse me."

He reached for the telephone and spoke into the mouthpiece, "Will you find out what's the delay? Call the committee and ask if they've left and when, and let me know."

He hung up.

"I think I should leave," I suggested uncertainly. "I've stayed more than an hour, and your people will be here any minute."

He gestured impatiently. "Now which field do you think you'd like to work in? Administration? Business? The arts? You're not qualified for any of these? Half of the people sitting there and drawing big salaries aren't either. Please, pick. I want to get your career started . . ."

The phone rang. He picked up the receiver and listened. "They're not coming?" he finally said, his hard face growing stony. "Was any reason given? No? . . . Thank you." He held the receiver as though he would crush it. Then he replaced it gently.

"Oh, Anna," he said with a near groan. And after a pause, "For a moment there, I thought, how wonderful, now you and I can have the rest of the afternoon and the evening for ourselves. But I guess I'll have to drive back into town. We'll make it another time? Meanwhile, think about what sort of job you would like . . ."

He sounded distracted, his lids were swollen, and the hand with which he poured himself a hooker of Scotch seemed unsure.

In the weeks that followed, his name disappeared entirely from press, radio, television. Since mention of it had always been infrequent, most people didn't notice; but those who could read the intricate daily barometer of our news media began to draw their conclusions from the silence.

I refused to accept these for a long time. He wasn't the type to fall without a crash that would reverberate through the country, I told myself and whoever would listen to me; besides, I believed I had evidence to the contrary. It was as though I had suddenly been handed an open sesame—I was offered the choice of half a dozen desirable positions at salaries exceeding anything I dared hope; my children were whizzed off to vacation camps of the finest sort; I was practically forced to accept a cure for an imagined illness in one of our better spas; in government offices, at the police, at the bank I no longer had to wait for hours, plead with subalterns or submit to humiliating questions but was treated with a courtesy that was almost embarrassing. I wanted to thank B., but we somehow missed one another. I waited at the fence, but nothing moved at his bungalow; the two or three times I heard he had been there I happened to be busy in town.

Fall had set in when I returned from my cure. Though I was rested and had gained weight, I felt dissatisfied and nervous and took the first bus to the country. I didn't bother to change clothes; I dropped my suitcase in the cottage and hurried to my seat at the fence. There was something desolate about the view that offered itself; the rain-sodden clouds added to the impression but they weren't the cause of it; the garden was untended, the flowers were dead, wilted shrubs were being engulfed by weeds, some of the terracing had begun to sag, the door to the guards' bungalow stood open and creaked each time a gust of wind moved it on its hinges.

I don't know what drove me: I climbed the fence. I tore my stockings at the wattles; I heard my skirt rip as it got caught; my hand was scratched badly and bled. I hastened up the serpentine path and stood breathless, on the flagstone terrace. The lake was an angry grey, the hills beyond capped in fog.

I started at his steps behind me.

"When did you come, Anna?" he asked.

I turned. His eyes were sunk in their sockets, his mouth had shrunk into a bitter, downward curve.

"A few minutes ago," I told him. "How long have you been here?"

"Couple of days."

The door to the guards' bungalow creaked again.

"Alone?"

"Alone."

I followed him indoors. His bedding lay, crumpled, on the couch; the copper sink was piled with unwashed dishes; the table was cluttered with empty bottles, cigarette butts, crusts of bread; in the fireplace the ashes were piled high—he had been burning papers.

I wanted to start creating some order; he waved me off. He shoved a drink at me and made me drink it and asked after the children. He wanted to know how I was getting along and seemed pleased with my report.

"You look fine," he said. "Filled out a bit. A new woman."

I tried to hide my shredded stockings under my torn skirt.

"I thought you would come," he said. "I've got some business to attend to. But I waited for you."

"How kind of you," I said, "I have so much to thank you for."

He laughed, a brief, hoarse, laugh. "That's the last I could do."

"The last . . ." The pieces of the picture fell into place.

He rose and stepped behind the chair in which I sat and put his hand on my hair.

"But how come?" I asked helplessly.

He stroked my forehead and temples; then his fingertips lost themselves at the back of my neck. I should have moved away from him, but I couldn't. I was inundated by currents outside my control; I shivered and felt my skin respond to his touch. I tried to recall what Tonda had told me of him. I thought of his hands closing around my throat.

"How come?" he repeated, caressing my shoulders. "They need a scapegoat, someone to throw to the people, someone to point the finger at: 'He's responsible! For the depredations and the hangings, for the fears and the terror, for the scarcities and the bureaucracy, for whatever ails you! But, see, we are kicking him out, we're exposing him! Look at him! We disrobed him, he is naked! Spit on him! Hit him! Kill him!'"

He stepped around the chair and knelt down before me.

"Oh, Anna," he groaned.

He took my hands and covered them with kisses.

"You mustn't," I said. "Pavel . . ."

He looked up at me with a despair that shook me.

"Why don't you fight back?" I said, though I felt it was hopeless. "If you are guilty, they're as guilty as you. They can't deny they knew. Whose decisions did you carry out? Your own, entirely?"

"And who will listen? Do you think Jan Vejner didn't cry out, or any of the others?" He buried his face in my lap. "Anna, Anna . . ."

Never in my life had a man really needed me; now this one did. Of all men, this one . . .

He raised his head, his face a grimace. "But I'll fool them. They're primitive. They think that by sacrificing me they can save their own skins. I'll leave them with nothing to wash their hands in . . ."

I stroked his face. The grimace gave way to an attempt at a smile.

"And new people will come," he said. "People with clean hands, to build what I once dreamed of building—bright, beautiful and in justice . . ."

He rose. He picked me up as though I were a small child and carried me in his arms across the room and lowered me on to the couch. "This once, Anna," he begged, "let's live."

I suffered his fingers ripping my clothes off. I suffered his hurting me. I desperately wanted it to work. But what cursed quirk had made him mention Jan Vejner! I lay there and listened to his moans and tried to accommodate him and felt him tear me, and something in the back of my mind kept repeating, *This week starts great, doesn't it?*

That was the last time I saw him alive.

On the week-end that followed they carried him past the cottage on an improvised stretcher. Someone had thrown a blanket over him that covered his head.

"You wouldn't want to look at him, Mrs. Ondrákova," said one of the villagers who had found him in the woods. "The bullet you know. And then the foxes were at him, and the crows."

I couldn't speak. I went to the fence and sat on my seat and stared across at the sloping garden that was turning back into wilderness. The picture windows in the bungalow seemed opaque with the grey of November; huge square eyes gone blind.

I heard someone call me, several people, in fact. The thick-necked young men had invaded my property. "Here she is!" said one, and turning to me, "Would you follow me?"

They escorted me back to my cottage. The man my children had christened Comrade Houndtooth was waiting for me. "We have a few questions to ask you, Mrs. Ondráková," he said quite civilly, "concerning the deceased Pavel B."

But what could I tell him?

The Wachsmuth Syndrome

The Wachsmuth Syndrome

I knew there was something funny when I woke up. Something unaccustomed.

The typewriter stood on my desk exactly as I had left it, my pipes were lined up in their rack, my trousers lay over the chair where I had thrown them before going to bed.

It couldn't be the cognac. I drink a glass of cognac every night, for my circulation. Nor do I smoke pot, take hash, or go on LSD trips. Susan was here, let's see, on Monday; I keep to the golden rule. I haven't masturbated since I turned seventeen.

My sense of something being not quite as it should be persisted. I did feel uncomfortable sitting up, almost as though my centre of gravity had changed its location. Moving about presented a slight problem too: I was bottom-heavy, and some weight dragged at my chest. I scratched my beard.

Beard.

Where on earth was my beard?

I rushed to the mirror. That mirror, full-length, framed in

mahogany, was bought at a good store; I knew I could trust it. And I knew there was no other person in the room whose image could be reflected in the glass, just me.

Me?

A person can always be identified by his teeth. The teeth in the mirror were definitely mine; I saw the two inlays and the familiar bridgework. The nose also belonged to me, though it seemed a little less rugged than yesterday, and cuter. So were the eyebrows mine, and the eyes, greyish green, with yellow speckles in the irises.

My fingers trembled as I unbuttoned my pyjamas. The breasts in the mirror weren't bad as breasts go, with a pair of dandy nipples that would have interested me on another woman.

Another woman? . . . I was a man!

I reached down to my crotch.

Jesus!

I nearly tore my pyjama trousers pulling them down. I looked. I took a second look. It couldn't be true. Not that the thing I had owned had been out of the ordinary in size or shape and an object of special admiration on the part of Susan or any of the other girls, but it had served, and I had liked having it. For a moment I had the wild notion that some mad surgeon had operated on me during the night, without my permission, and I felt for the scar. There was no scar. There was just the well-known aperture.

Dr. Tauber was the family physician.

Dr. Tauber had brought me into this world. My mother used to delight in telling me how Dr. Tauber came into the room, stepped to her bedside, and proclaimed, "It's a boy. A very fine little boy!" Dr. Tauber therefore must know what I did or did not have to start with.

Getting dressed proved a bit awkward. I had a bra somewhere that one of Susan's predecessors had left, but it proved too small. My derriere barely fit in the seat of my trousers, my jacket bulged suspiciously in front. I decided to wear an overcoat despite the warm, sunny weather.

"My," said Dr. Tauber, "have you changed! Goes to show you why the police frown on this beard fashion. You take off your beard, you're a changed man."

"Changed man," I said. "I wish it were just that."

He dug with his finger in his ear as though he had water on his eardrum. I noticed that my voice had slid up by nearly an octave; I was a contralto.

"Doc," I said, "I'm in trouble."

He looked worried and puzzled.

"You've got to help me, Doc. There's something, I don't know how to tell you, but it's pretty terrible."

"Now, now," he said, "it won't be that bad. I pulled you through the German measles and through the mumps; I set several of your bones; I cured that nasty little infection of yours; I'll try to take care of your present complaint. Open your mouth."

"Doc," I said, "it isn't just the voice." I started undressing. "It's all over me."

"What's all over you?"

I stood before him.

His face changed colour. His mouth opened and closed like a sick fish's.

"I told you I was in bad trouble," I said in an attempt to help him over his shock.

"Madam," he said when he could talk again, "I'm sure I don't know what you intended pulling on me by impersonating a young friend of mine, a *male* friend. If . . . ."

"Look, Doc," I interrupted gently, "see the scar on my arm? You made that incision when I was three months old. It saved my life. Now look at my foot, no, the other one. The third toe overlaps the fourth. You know I was born with that; it runs in the family."

He nodded.

I told him a few more things which only he and I could know. I mentioned my teeth; and if those weren't enough, I said, the army must have a set of fingerprints which would prove that I was I.

"But in the army you were a man," he said, pained.

"And now I appear to be a woman. That's why I've come to you."

He approached me hesitantly and felt my mammae. They were genuine enough, none of that silicone or whatever they use on a plastic job.

"But if you are what you are now"—he grew excited—"and if you were what we know you were, then this is . . . stupendous! It's unique! It'll do to medical science what the splitting of the atom did to physics. We must take you to Wachsmuth!"

I felt distinctly apprehensive at the prospect of playing to medical science the part which the first split atom has played to physics.

"Wachsmuth is your man. Every hermaphrodite in the city has been through his hands."

"But I don't think I'm an hermaphrodite," I mentioned.

"What you are is up to Wachsmuth to determine. Maybe we'll have to find a new term. Maybe there's a complete new development of which you're the first example: a new Adam."

"A new Eve," I said. "May I dress now?"

Professor Anatol Wachsmuth, M.D., D.S., D.Litt., etc., was cool and dispassionate, a man whose scientific approach to things seemed both to have formed his character and marked his face. Yet I saw him wax tense as Dr. Tauber got deeper into my story.

Dr. Tauber stuck to the facts, leaving the conclusions to his famous colleague. Professor Wachsmuth asked a few brief questions: had I been getting any hormones, orally or by injection? Had I during the last month consumed anything out of the ordinary, any foreign, especially oriental foods or potions that were previously unknown to me? Had I to my knowledge been exposed to radiation, X-ray, cosmic, or otherwise? Had I recently noticed any undue growth, or shrinkage of any part of myself? Any new and unusual desires, not necessarily sexual?

I denied every one of these in a firm but distinctly feminine voice. Professor Wachsmuth apparently had anticipated my answers; he motioned me to his obstetrical chair. Aware of my anxiety at my first vaginal, Dr. Tauber held my hand while the Professor explored all those new gadgets of mine which up to date I had only encountered elsewhere.

"Everything complete," Professor Wachsmuth said finally, "and not a trace of the male. Of course, we still have to have her—I mean his—hormone status."

He called in his nurse and told her to tap me for 10 cc.; the test tube was to be kept separate, he himself would attend to the analyses. And while the nurse perforated my vein and drew out my nice, dark red blood, he began a rapid colloquy with Dr. Tauber, something about devising a method to determine if my psyche had mutated along with my organism.

That was the least of my concerns. The questions that moved me were of a more practical nature. Should I continue to impersonate my old self, for instance, should I try to act the man I no longer was? Any public toilet would expose me. But if I started wearing skirts and high-heeled shoes and let my hair grow, I would lose many of my clients; also I hated the patronising manner certain judges displayed towards female attorneys. There was no end of problems, down to learning how to button myself the other way around.

The two medical men had come to some conclusion. Professor Wachsmuth waited till I was fully clothed to give his opinion. "Your case is entirely new in my experience. I'll once more check through related literature, but I'm fairly sure there'll be nothing. Don't misunderstand: the matter is by no means hopeless. As soon as we have your hormone status, we'll design a tentative course of treatment; the definite treatment will have to wait on our finding the cause of your mutation. I strongly suspect your genes, you know, the little things that carry the coded information which determines growth and character of your cells. A change in your genes may have affected your gonads. But a whole complex of other factors must have entered the picture to bring about so radical a mutation in so short a time. We shall need some extended research, consultations, more tests. We'll call in a top biologist, a geneticist, a gynecologist, a biophysicist, other men as required. We won't hurt you. We'll just ask you to hold yourself in readiness for further examinations. Of course, if you prefer our not doing anything, if you wish to stay what you have become—from what I can see, you are now a perfectly healthy woman—I can't force my services on you. But in the interest of science and in your own interest, madam—I mean, sir—I wish you would help us to get to the bottom of this extraordinary, this singular, this most promising new phenomenon which I should like to call the Wachsmuth syndrome."

A comparatively obscure item in the Journal of Applied Sexology set the ball rolling.

The journal reported Prof. Anatol Wachsmuth, M.D., D.S., D.Litt., etc., the well-known sexologist and hormone specialist, as having mentioned to several distinguished colleagues that he had found a complete case of spontaneous mutation (male to female) in a fully grown member of a species of higher vertebrates. Prof. Wachsmuth was preparing a paper on the case which was considered singular.

A few days later the local daily carried a front page story referring to the item in the *Journal of Applied Sexology*. The paper added that the species of higher vertebrates in question was in fact the species homo sapiens, and that its mutated member was a respected young member of the bar whose name was being withheld, but who was known to the editor. In the adjoining two columns they printed a photograph of me, a black oblong superimposed on part of my face to avoid possible legal action, and what they called an artist's conception of myself in a bikini after my mutation. Several paragraphs set in italics followed the story. They were written by the scientific correspondent, who spoke highly of the past achievements of Prof. Anatol Wachsmuth, M.D., D.S., D.Litt., etc., and predicted that his discovery of the new mutation syndrome, to be aptly called the Wachsmuth syndrome, would immortalise his fame. An editorial on the fourth page hinted broadly that the Wachsmuth syndrome, unless it remained restricted to the case of Mr. (or was it now Miss?) Dash Dash Dash, might well take care of the population explosion.

The joker who wrote that should have known how close he would be to the truth.

Things happened then.

It didn't take ten minutes for the rest of the papers, for the news services, for television and radio to detect my name and address. The telephone started ringing and never stopped. In the lobby of my apartment house lines formed at the reception desk and in front of the elevators. Friends I hadn't seen in years casually dropped by to inquire how I felt now that I had mutated. Newsmen fought each other for a question at me; photographers begged, Mister, give us some cheesecake, that's fine, that's a good boy, God bless you. One television station actually hired a fire truck and ran out the ladder outside my window to get some footage of me *en déshabillé*, brushing my teeth. Some vicious voices that spoke of a giant hoax were silenced by the sworn statements of Dr. Tauber and by the public display of my army fingerprints, which were irrefutable. I received offers from motion picture companies wanting me to star in the most daring films, from television chains willing to pay any amount for anything from a half hour show to a series, from some of our most eligible bachelors prepared to lead me to the altar, and from dirty-minded creatures of all ages suggesting the most outlandish games. I was offered a judgeship, the first female judge in the country to have been a male. I was invited to teach at the biggest universities. Women's clubs wrote that, as a new woman, I owed them a lecture on how it felt to be a woman. The women's liberation movement nominated me vice-president saying that, as a former man, I would have a particular appreciation of the disadvantages and discriminations from which women suffered. The Government considered sending me on an international goodwill mission: there were astronauts and cosmonauts by the dozen, but only one mutant. My glory reached its pinnacle when one of the most notorious underground organisations threatened to kidnap me. As the nation's most treasured individual, I was placed under 24-hour police guard.

But Wachsmuth was not satisfied. He grew increasingly moody, though I kept my appointments with him religiously.

"Your life belongs to science," he growled, "not to this circus. The whole world talks of the Wachsmuth syndrome. Do we have any idea of what it is, or why it comes about? And what of your genes? Have they changed? If so, how? You have learned to pronounce desoxyribonucleic acid without getting your tongue twisted, but do we know what effect, if any, it had on your sudden sex shift? There you are, a rather good-looking young woman with a male past: that's all we really know. But that we knew the day Dr. Tauber brought you into this office. . . ." He broke off. "Ah, you'll never understand."

But I thought I understood. Something in me had stirred, a feminine instinct.

But was I a woman? I mean, down in my heart?

The big colloquium which was to decide that ended in failure. There were those rows and rows of great men come from a number of countries—psychologists, psychiatrists, sexologists, what have you—myself and Professor Wachsmuth on the platform, and the press up on the gallery and the cameras grinding away, and they were asking me these embarrassing questions.

Maybe I should have told them one way or the other and been

done with it, but I honestly didn't know: did I still feel attracted to women, or had I a recent penchant for men? The thing with Susan was over: that much was fact. She had said she was willing to stick with me, but I felt I shouldn't take advantage of her loyalty. There had been a young liftboy who brought me a floral arrangement sent by an advertising agency: he suddenly blushed and asked if he just might kiss my cheek and I let him. But that was all. In all the rush and business in which I constantly was involved I simply hadn't had the opportunity to get any sort of feeling about a man or a woman.

"Gentlemen," I said after cutting a rather sad figure, "I'm afraid I can't make up my mind about that. I just know that none of you in this hall arouses anything in me."

That got me the laughs, but it didn't settle my problem. And I saw the deep frown on Professor Wachsmuth's face.

Suddenly my situation was altered.

A flash news bulletin burst upon the world: a Liverpool dockworker, Gus Emmett, had turned woman and was calling himself Gwendolyn. A few hours later the same thing was reported from Istanbul where a Turkish trumpeter named Hakim al Bülbül had changed sex. Further mutation stories emanated from Lima, Peru, and Bangalore in South India, but the cases referred to, a donkey driver and a practising guru, were not confirmed by serious medical authority.

At any rate, I no longer was the sole living specimen of the Wachsmuth syndrome. I can't say that I was unhappy. It's always a consolation to have fellowship in misfortune, if becoming a woman after some good years as a male may properly be called a misfortune. I wrote to Gwendolyn, offering my advice as a mutant of several months' experience. Gwendolyn wrote back gratefully and related some delightful anecdotes about the reaction of her dockworker friends to her new status. If I had known Turkish, I should have similarly written to Hakim al Bülbül; however I couldn't see myself exchanging confidences through a translator.

Professor Wachsmuth flew both to Liverpool and Istanbul. On his return he seemed depressed. The symptoms, he told me, were exactly as mine: the two men had turned into completely equipped females, shedding in the process every vestige of their one-time male appurtenances; the process itself remained a mystery since, just as in my case, it occurred during a deep, dreamless sleep.

The press and the commentators grew cautious. One mutant was a sensation, a freak, an object of public wonder. Three of them, or five if you trusted the reports from Peru and South India, gave cause for thought: not yet a matter of public concern, it was nothing to be brushed away lightly. The various scientific opinions on the origins and possible cures of the Wachsmuth syndrome were duly registered and their contradictory nature was noted with misgivings. If the medical men on whom the public relied were that much at odds, how was the average citizen to behave in the face of the new phenomenon?

A certain urgency manifested itself in the editorials and news comments when, on the Monday after Epiphany, a spate of reports appeared of fresh mutations in Norway and Italy, in South Africa and Brazil, in Ohio, Florida, Maine and Ontario, in Japan (two), on Bali and in Thailand, in Israel, in Iran, and in Morocco. The next day new cases were added from Finland, from Tyrol, from the Sudan, Southern France, Spain (one in Catalonia, one in Valladolid), from Mexico, Paraguay, Barbados, also from Pakistan (three), Honolulu, and Australia. Even in Iceland a glacier guide, a giant of a man, had suddenly turned female. He refused to wear women's clothes, though, and continued to affect a bass voice in the hope that with the return of summer his renowned masculinity would return as well.

Here was a new illness, opinion ran, if an illness it was. True, it didn't kill. True, it had not reached epidemic proportions. Its eeriness lay in its erratic behaviour: no predicting when, where, and whom it would hit. A man might peacefully fall asleep beside his lawfully wedded wife, to awake in the morning a member of the opposite sex. What this did to his family life, his job, his business was anybody's guess. But what of our medical science? Was the Wachsmuth syndrome beyond the power of our great doctors, our institutions of learning and research? And what about the governments? Billions were being spent on all sorts of things: why was there no international project to investigate the Wachsmuth syndrome; why was there not even an international scientific symposium on the subject? Did we want to wait until it was too late?

From the East came differing voices. Nothing in the faintest resembling the Wachsmuth syndrome had been noticed in the socialist countries, wrote *Literaturnaya Gazeta*, obviously this strange mutation of men into women was a symptom of capitalist degeneration, akin to public immorality and the widespread use of harmful drugs. *Literaturnaya Gazeta* changed its line when in Poland a number of Catholic monks turned into devout nuns, and when from Kazakstan, Estonia, Vladivostok, and Erivan reports trickled into Moscow of man-to-woman mutations in those areas. *Literaturnaya Gazeta* calmed its readers by declaring that the Wachsmuth syndrome in truth should be called the Bezymensky syndrome, after Professor Andrey Philippovich Bezymensky, who in the sixties of the past century had observed similar mutations in the Urals mining field.

Thus was the state of things when the avalanche broke loose.

I well remember that spring: never had the trees budded more beautifully, never had the sky seemed that high and that blue. But people were panicked. A few dozen cases per day of the Wachsmuth syndrome, spread over the globe, mushroomed to hundreds, then thousands, then tens of thousands. The thinning out of the male population on the streets of the cities, in the theatres, on buses, trains, planes, was frightening to observe. The remaining men became shy, introspective; they had something about them of the tired old flies that crawl across the window sill on a winter's day. Wives, suddenly widowed by mutation, tried to keep up a semblance of married life; but as their boy children turned into girls, the institution of the family assumed a new, perplexing character. Elsewhere orgiastic parties were being thrown at which the few males the hostesses could procure were shamelessly exploited. Several governments thought of introducing a system of rationing men, but the rapid increase of the mutation rate outdated every quota before it could become law.

Science was helpless. In their desperation, men tried their own remedies. Some shut themselves off in garrets, caves, lonely mountain huts, preferring life as recluses to life as women. Others believed in garlic, in frequent massages of their pertinent parts, in curare, in the waters of certain springs. Mass pilgrimages were undertaken to Lourdes, Mecca, Benares, Zagorsk, Lhasa; but of every thousand male pilgrims setting out, it was calculated that an average of three hundred returned as mutants. Writers treated the new subject and its attending complications in film, on the stage, in stories and novels; several authors who began their works as men finished them as women, which offered to critics and students fine material for comparative studies of male and female writing.

The news media which initially published daily mutation figures based on representative sample areas ceased that practice; they restricted themselves to reporting just the most prominent cases, such as that of a Greek shipping magnate who, having mutated, blew himself up together with the entire island he owned. But this was an extreme. On the whole, once a man had mutated, he took his fate like a man and tried to make the best of his new face and figure. A number of people told me they even derived a certain satisfaction from seeing a hefty girl, obviously a mutant, handle a bulldozer or climb the mast of a high tension line or bounce a recalcitrant male out of the corner bar where the poor fellow had gone to drown his apprehensions.

Though they were patently senseless, I kept up my visits to Professor Wachsmuth.

He now lived as under a curse, as though he had invented the syndrome that carried his name. He had been the centre of hopes that some means might be found of combating the dreaded mutation; as these hopes dwindled and the jokes whose butt he was grew stale, he retired more and more to his serums and his slides.

That day it wasn't the nurse who opened the door. "Why!" I said. "Isn't this . . ."

"Call me Agnes." The Professor drew me into the office and motioned me to the chair on which I always sat. "It's happened. Last night. I expected it for the longest time: why should I be exempt from my own syndrome. I had hoped I'd feel some of it, observe, make notes. But no, I slept through it. How do I look?"

"Great!" Professor Anatol Wachsmuth had been a fine figure of a man, youthful for his years, well-knit; some of that had transferred into the female. "Perhaps, if you combed your hair a little differently . . . May I?" I led the Professor to the mirror, took out my pocket comb and did a few things. "Now, isn't that better?"

"You know, I'll have to learn so much from you."

We sat down on the couch. Professor Wachsmuth held my hands.

"I've been thinking last night, before I—before I mutated. Wachsmuth, I said, Nature is Nature. Remember all those little bugs that we used to kill by penicillin? Suddenly there appeared a strain that was penicillin resistant. Wachsmuth, I said, somewhere on this globe, right this minute, there must grow one gene that is mutation resistant: all we have to do is find it."

"Isn't that a pretty large order?" I said. "And if you found it, wouldn't it be too late—for you, for me?"

"So much in this world comes too late." Professor Wachsmuth caressed my fingers. "I've been meaning to tell you, dear. I've loved you all along. I fell in love with you the day you came here the first time. . . ."

"Anatol!" I blushed.

"Agnes," the Professor corrected. "That's just it. Too late."

I kissed her, the chaste kiss of one mutant kissing another of her kind.

Those who had theorised that mass mutation would end the prevalent social conflicts were mistaken. On the contrary, as men faded from the picture, as radical groups and the forces of law both became increasingly feminised, class and radical clashes grew increasingly vindictive. As for the current wars, they just went on.

But a whole complex of conflicts entirely unknown in recorded history arose between the OWs (original women) and the MWs (mutation women). The OWs, being of pure, unmutated sex, claimed not only superiority but seniority. The positions previously held by men in business and in the professions, plus the former male privileges, now were rightfully theirs; let those sexual bastards, the MWs, take their turn as cleaning women, kindergarteners, nurses, typists, receptionists, and bunny girls. The MWs on the other hand held that by training and experience, by their very masculine past, they were entitled to stick to the jobs they had held as men: if it was a man's world no longer, it was not going to be a woman's world either. Without formally organising, the MWs functioned like a mafia, furthering each other and protecting each other against OW competition. "Oh, you're one of us, too?" or a few casual words like it would suffice to assure the MW of the sorority's assistance. This in turn caused the OWs to take counter-measures. An embittered struggle ensued, a new sort of civil war which was fought in the jungle of day-to-day life and which was the more terrible for the fact that both contending sides consisted of women.

On the surface little of that showed. The political institutions created by the rapidly vanishing males somehow continued functioning, much as a wrist-watch ticks on though its owner lies dead of the stroke. The British, as usual, made the smoothest transition; of course they were ruled by a Queen long before the appearance of the Wachsmuth syndrome; Her Majesty now was married to the Duchess of Edinburgh. Chairman Mao, in China, simply became Chairwoman Mao: all feminine virtues and wisdom were immediately ascribed to her and a number of excellent Chinese recipes were added to the Little Red Book. On the day the General Secretary of the Communist Party of the Soviet Union turned into a rather ponderous elderly lady, the MWs took control of the Politbureau: a communiqué was issued in which the continuity of Soviet policy was stressed and all governments were assured that the USSR would scrupulously hold to its treaty obligations. There was some constitutional debate in the United States because a daily decreasing number of enfeebled males protested that they never elected a woman President, but the Vice-President had mutated nearly three weeks before the President and the opposition could offer no proper substitute for the chief executive. In a new election, which some demanded, the men would have been heavily outnumbered; so the call for it was quietly dropped.

By and by it dawned on people that the Wachsmuth syndrome meant the end of the human race. As in the natural course of events women and mutants aged, died, and were buried, as less and less infants were born and those of the male sex mutated within the first ten days of their young lives, people began to long back to the days when the public talk was of the population explosion, and would the earth be able to hold our progeny? The saurians, whose huge skeletons enlivened our museums of natural history, were thoughtfully remembered; a time was predicted when the remains of the strange bipeds who once roamed the earth and burned and bombed it as the spirit moved them would be displayed to interested groups of termites, or night owls, or crocodiles; and wry tribute was paid to the long-mutated editorial writer who had warned of the development when there was only one sample of a live mutant, myself.

Deep gloom spread over the globe: Gotterdammerung was obviously at hand. Churches, mosques, temples, tabernacles filled with wailing OWs and MWs; preachers called for penitence; public officials for law and order. There was no general relaxation of morals because there was nothing to relax your morals with. A famous poetess wrote some lines to her mutant friend that were set to music and played in every discotheque:

The two of us
Dearie
Will be the last
So let's de—e—e—e—part
Together

And then word reached Professor Wachsmuth of a boy baby born in the small town of Koetzschenbroda, in a European country called the German Democratic Republic, who refused to mutate. His proud mother called him Otto. His father had mutated shortly after begetting him, so Otto was in a sense a posthumous child.

I never saw Agnes that excited. "That's it!" she cried as she paced her laboratory, "that's my resistant strain!" She took the next plane to East Berlin and reached Koetzschenbroda in due time. There, in an old-fashioned house that breathed *Gemuetlichkeit*, lay Otto in his crib, happily gurgling and sucking his big toe.

Agnes described him to me, her face wreathed in a motherly smile: a fat, good-natured baby—"and he's got everything!" She showed me the pictures she had taken for the paper she would write and soon publish. "It's the fulfilment of my life," she proclaimed, "the second Wachsmuth syndrome!"

I looked at the photos with a certain melancholy: once I, too, had been like Otto. But I had no right to complain. If those little things I saw there survived, the human race would go on, with all that implied.

The article on Baby Otto by Prof. Agnes Wachsmuth, M.D., D.S., D.Litt., etc., in the *Journal of Applied Sexology* proved a bombshell. The front page of the biggest tabloid in town blossomed out with the giant-sized headline RACE SAVED, and a picture of

Otto's saving equipment. The paper stated editorially that apologies were due to Professor Wachsmuth who had been made to suffer so much for the sake of her science but who in the nick of time had come forth with the answer to humanity's problem: the second Wachsmuth syndrome. The same issue of the paper contained a special supplement on the geography, economy, politics and cultural life of the German Democratic Republic; the only country on earth which could boast of a male. The Government there wisely prevented little Otto from being victimised as I was by a sensation-hungry press and by the usual capitalist business hyenas. Otto and his mother were efficiently screened off; a commission of medical women and educators was named to assure Otto a normal childhood; his entire future was planned and parcelled out, the socialist countries naturally having first choice. But that share of Otto's future natural resources which was to be made available for export to the West proved sufficiently valuable to turn the East Mark into one of the most sought-after currencies.

The secret worry of everyone concerned is of course that Otto might not last, that by some quirk of fate he too might mutate, dashing all the proud hopes that are set on him. But to judge by the daily bulletins issued by the governmental commission he still is complete and growing lustily.

At this writing, that is.

The Creator and
The Commissars

The Creator and The Commissars

by J. Robert Moskin

An Encounter with Stefan Heym

Stefan Heym's tortured, successful career—born in response to Nazism, nurtured in democracy, grounded in Marxism—mirrors the political traumas of our time. His novels have been best sellers, in turn, in Britain, in the United States, the GDR, and West Germany. Today, he is the paterfamilias of an East German literary revival little recognised in the West.

Before I met him, I assumed Heym was a survivor—one of those adroit, rubbery people who zigzag to stay afloat. But, in talking through a long afternoon in Frankfurt's Intercontinental Hotel, where he was visiting from East Berlin, I found that this bulky, affable, articulate man of 59 has an iron conviction that, despite the tyrannies of politics, a writer must speak out.

Born in Chemnitz (now Karl-Marx-Stadt), Heym as a schoolboy wrote leftist political poetry, was beaten up by Nazis, and thrown out of school. When Hitler roared to power in 1933, the 20-year-old Heym fled to Prague. Two years later, he moved on to America and was soon editing an antifascist, German-language weekly in New York. His first novel, Hostages, *became a best seller and a film.*

During World War II, Heym served as the GI editor of a United States' army of occupation newspaper in Germany and won a commission in the field and a Bronze Star. In 1945, he refused an order to write an anti-Soviet editorial and was discharged. Back in the United States, he kept writing. During the Korean War, he sent off his medal to President Eisenhower in protest and, "because of the persecutions" of the McCarthy period, left in 1952 for East Germany.

As a novelist, Heym won the GDR's top award, the National Prize. Then his political outspokenness got him in trouble. Now he is unpublished at home but, paradoxically, still allowed to publish in the West and to travel and earn hard currency there. His novel, The King David Report, *was very well received in Great Britain (where it was published by Hodder and Stoughton), and in West Germany. Heinrich Böll, the West German Nobel Laureate, in a review in* Der Spiegel, *praised the book, its author, and his courage.*

Still a dedicated Marxist, Heym criticises the Communist leaders when he disagrees with them. How can an outspoken non-person survive and create under a regime that would like to suppress all dissent? Stefan Heym fields such questions with surprising candour . . .

QUESTION: Is creativity flourishing in the German Democratic Republic today?

HEYM: Yes, and I think the very restrictions we have contribute to that. People are thinking much more. [In the West] a lot of nonsense is being published, but [in the GDR] the writers who express the spirit of their time try to get at things in a way that is acceptable to the publishers—let's call them publishers—and sometimes they bring out books that are really alive, significant.

And now—and this is a new thing—a real literary discussion

has started. Of course, it must be seen in political context; you have to know how to read it and where to find it. A part of the leadership wants not just to polish up the image of the GDR but genuinely wants a literature that is alive.

Q: It's dangerous, isn't it, to encourage "alive" literature?

HEYM: It depends on whether your society is elastic enough to accept criticism. If it's brittle and weak, then, of course, an alive literature might be a dangerous thing. I had a discussion with one of the more powerful men about this question. We talked about the danger that the writer represents in certain situations, and he mentioned Hungary and Czechoslovakia. And I said that it wasn't the writers who were at the root of it. The writers only reflected what was. So, it's not the mirror you should smash if you don't like your face.

Q: What reaction did you get to that?

HEYM: A smile. They know it's true. But, of course, literature becomes alive, and then—boom!—something political happens as a reaction. That's the way it [seems to appear] to them—a conditioned reflex, more or less. Therefore, the distrust towards literature.

My feeling is that changes must be made, but these changes cannot be made in out-and-out opposition to the leadership of the party or to the Soviet Union. The changes will come about because socialism is developing. And we must be active in helping these changes to come about. That is, or should be, the position of responsible writers in the socialist world. I'm trying to act along those lines.

Q: Isn't it true that the Establishment in almost any society feels endangered by the creative act?

HEYM: That's right. You see it in history all the time. If in a capitalistic country the political situation becomes critical, it also will take steps against the creative artist, the writer. Take the case of the Hollywood Ten [during the McCarthy era]. That is not so long ago in the United States. And if something [becomes] seriously wrong there again, they would do the same thing. But [such an act] is a sign of the weakness of the society. And I believe that the socialist society is not as weak as all that.

Q: Then it is rather the Establishment's vision of its own society?

HEYM: Its own insecurity. Exactly. It's a question of how the Establishment sees its own society.

Q: And you get into the question of time. You couldn't have the Hollywood Ten today in the States. You might have it tomorrow, but not today.

HEYM: Not today. And you couldn't have out-and-out persecution of writers in the GDR either today. To wit, I am here. And nothing has happened to any writer in the GDR, even to those who were very sharply attacked. They run around freely.

Q: One East German writer who has been published in the U.S. is Christa Wolf. How do you see her?

HEYM: I see in Christa Wolf a sincere writer of great courage. At the eleventh plenary session [of the Central Committee] I think she was the only member who got up and opposed the attacks on her colleagues. She lost her position in the Central Committee. I think she's a person of great integrity. She has now turned to stories that concern the inner life of people.

Q: Your most recent books have not been published in the GDR.

HEYM: My last three books have not been published in the GDR.

Q: Why are you out of favour?

HEYM: Two years after I settled in the GDR, we had a counter-revolutionary putsch. I wrote a novel about that. I felt it should be published, but a number of important people in the GDR, to whom I showed the manuscript, thought it should not be published. I accepted their opinion and withdrew the manuscript. Today I'm quite glad about it because I feel that the novel did not give a complete and rounded picture of the events, which were very complicated.

In the years immediately following 1953, I published a column called "Plain Talk". I picked up sore spots, let's say, and wrote about them. I aroused the opposition of a number of important people who felt themselves criticised or attacked. And in 1956 the column closed down.

Later on, I began to think about literary life in the GDR. I wrote a number of articles and gave a number of speeches at meetings of international socialist writers. My position was a little different from the official ideologies. Gradually a conflict came about.

Then I began to write historical novels: the first one about the revolution of [1848]. That book was published in the GDR, but the next novel, on [Ferdinand] Lassalle, not. I think the real reason was that Lassalle is a non-person of the working-class movement. He had a falling-out with Marx. I considered Lassalle on the basis of this question: How [much] can you work together with the enemy in order to achieve your progressive aims? He had written a play about this.

My book on Lassalle was published in England under the title *Uncertain Friend.* After Lassalle's death, Engels wrote to Marx that Lassalle was a great character but that he was an uncertain friend and in all likelihood would have become an enemy.

The other thing [about Lassalle] that interested me was the question of the one-man dictatorship in the working-class movement. Was that just an aberration in Stalin's time? Or was the possibility of a one-man dictatorship built into the structure of the working-class movement?

Q: Did you decide this was built in?

HEYM: Not as a necessity but as a possibility. So, I don't know whether this was why the book wasn't published in the GDR.

The next book that was not published is my novelette on Defoe. In 1702, he anonymously published a pamphlet about the right way to deal with dissenters. For that, he was arrested, tried, put in the pillory. There was a demonstration for him, much to the annoyance of the government, and I wrote about this little episode.

Q: You were touching, in historical terms, issues that are not totally dead.

HEYM: History has great relevance to our time. It doesn't mean that I will always write historical novels. *The King David Report* is the last of them for a while. It is the story of the exercise of power and the succession of a despot who comes to power in a revolution.

Q: With a relevance again of some kind?

HEYM: Well, any revolution is relevant to another revolution.

Q: What is your relationship as a writer to the society you are living in and not being published in?

HEYM: I think not being published is a temporary thing. In my mind, it represents a fear that if people begin to think about their own problems, they might be less amenable to being good citizens—which I think is ridiculous. I think the more that people are made to think the better it is for socialism. It is not good to consider people as children who cannot be told the truth.

Q: Is dissent welcomed?

HEYM: I think this is one of our shortcomings. Stalin himself once wrote that if you don't listen to criticism from the people, they will criticise you by uprisings. Thinking and criticism should be encouraged instead of discouraged. It would make people better socialists.

Q: Did you find that this view is persuasive in your society?

HEYM: Definitely. I feel that many people inside the party and also in the leading circles of the party believe that the old ways are no longer effective. But, of course, they are not yet clear about what must be changed and the process of change. It is necessary to find a way of changing the mode of operation without the risk of violence. Oh, a risk you will always have—but avoiding mishaps. As in Hungary, for instance. Or as in Czechoslovakia. I don't think that [the Russians] planned [to] invade.

Q: What was the mishap there?

HEYM: Some of the Czech things got out of hand and, of course, the invasion was a panic reaction—but an understandable one.

Q: I had the impression that attitudes in the GDR have changed since 1971 with the new leadership.

HEYM: Yes, definitely they have changed.

Q: And your non-personship goes back beyond that?

HEYM: Yes, yes. That went back to the infamous eleventh plenary session, in which a number of writers were pilloried in the GDR. From then on, we were non-persons.

It didn't succeed in my case because I was an established writer. I continued to write and continued to publish. Also everybody in the GDR knows, I think, that I'm not antisocialist or anticommunist or one of *them*, but I reserve the right to have differences of opinion, which is honest enough.

Q: Have they the power to shut you up?

HEYM: Well, of course, they could take violent means. They could put me in gaol, but this is not the time for that, and it would also be very difficult to do. You cannot try an author now for what he writes. You can't do it in the GDR; you can't do it in other socialist countries. If I would organise something, maybe it would be different.

At first, with the Lassalle book, they tried to take an administrative measure. They fined me 300 marks for publishing the book in the West without official permission. They couldn't charge more than 300 marks without trying me in court, and that would have been very awkward for them. I would have spoken out in court, and it would have been very embarrassing. But they haven't pulled that little stunt again. On the contrary, I'm permitted to go [to the West] to speak about a book that is not yet published in the GDR. It *is* a contradictory situation. It's a sign of the times.

Q: How do you explain it?

HEYM: Well, hell, I don't know how to explain it really. I'm not inside the skulls of the people who decide that. I apply and then I learn whether I may go or not. But I think that it is a wise decision on their part. If they don't let me go, that probably would arouse comment. They would like to avoid that.

Q: What happens when you write a book like *The King David Report?* Do you submit it for publication?

HEYM: Well, I have a publisher in Leipzig who printed my [earlier] books. They are now putting out a new edition of my [1848] revolutionary novel, and they, if anyone, should be printing the three titles that have not yet appeared. They know the books, of course. And I'm waiting for them to call me and say, please, we are interested in the books. But they haven't done so.

Q: You don't send them the manuscript. Then it's not an active act of rejection?

HEYM: The Lassalle was actually rejected.

Q: With a reason?

HEYM: The reason was given: no paper. And the Defoe book was rejected because it might be misunderstood. And I didn't bother to ask for an explanation on the David. Why should I put them on the spot?

Q: Let's turn to the future. What do you see happening in the GDR—literarily?

HEYM: I think that especially among the younger people there is a need to express the conflicts of the times and the development of their own lives. You can't stop that, as uncomfortable as it might be to certain diehards. And my prediction for the literature of the GDR is a very good one. I think our attitude should *not* be defensive. We should not try to create a mental wall around us. We should create literature and art that's attractive to the West. Then we don't have to worry about Western influence and there'll be an Eastern influence. We have the talents to create that.

Q: What about your own literary future?

HEYM: I will return to contemporary subjects. Also I want to do some short stories. I did a short story recently and it came out in

Playboy. I haven't seen *Playboy*. You see, when they sent *Playboy* to me, it didn't get through, because they don't permit naked girls to go through the mail in the GDR. I didn't get my copy, but I got the clipping.

Q: What is your prospect of becoming an ex-nonperson?

HEYM: Who am I—a prophet? But I think that things are looking up. For the first time I am being printed again in the GDR with a new short story in the magazine of the Academy of Arts. I think that the Lassalle, at least, might be able to get through in the near future.

Q: With changes?

HEYM: I want to change it because it was too long in its original form—but no political changes. No, that I wouldn't do. Hell, no. If they ask me, then I will say forget it.

Q: Do you feel you walk a tightrope?

HEYM: Yes, but I feel comfortable walking it. I've done it for a long time. It's a pretty wide tightrope.

Q: You are pretty expert at walking it?

HEYM: I don't know how expert I am, but I think: What can happen to me? Nothing. They don't print me anyhow. And secondly, I'm not saying anything against socialism. Socialism is my thing. I am a socialist.

Q: Are you a member of the party?

HEYM: No.

Q: Have you been in the past?

HEYM: No. But I'm not saying anything wrong. All I do is criticise certain features or certain persons. They deserve to be criticised, and I'll be damned if I will keep my mouth shut. I don't criticise for the sake of criticism. If a subject comes up, then I'll treat it in the way in which I feel it should be treated and let the chips fall. Or when I give a speech on literature, I'll say what I think and not what somebody else wants me to say. That's the extent of my tightrope walking.

Of course, I weigh my words because in this world words can

be misinterpreted. I try to speak as carefully as I can so I cannot be misinterpreted, but that's true for anyone.

Q: You seem able to perform with more independence than I thought was possible in this society.

HEYM: Yes, because I take the liberty of performing.

Q: You mean the *courage* to perform?

HEYM: I didn't want to use that word because . . . You may want to use it but *I do not*. Don't quote me as saying that I have the courage to do it. I take the liberty of doing it. That's all there is to it, and anybody can.

Q: Anybody can? In the Soviet Union some who have taken the liberty have ended up in camps.

HEYM: Yes, that's true. But first of all, I live in the German Democratic Republic and not in the Soviet Union. Secondly, you have Solzhenitsyn who does not end up in a camp. Okay, he was, but that was a different time. And you have other authors who have spoken out, and you have a lot of authors who have published things.

In the GDR, I don't think anybody at the moment would get put in jail for writing something. While in the Soviet Union this happens. But there is a greater latitude for expression in Soviet literature and in Soviet films than there is at present in the GDR. I've seen Soviet films that I would consider audacious in the GDR But it's changing. We are progressing.

Q: You've been a socialist a long time.

HEYM: Longer than I care to remember. Once I was a real idealist and rather foolish. I didn't know anything. But now I've thought about it, I've had conflicts, I've had fights and all that, and I'm still a socialist. I know it is the right thing, despite all the disadvantages, all the mistakes, all the stupidities. After all, it's a long time in building. The world doesn't change overnight. . . .

Have you anything else you'd like to ask?

Q: Can I communicate with you directly at home?

HEYM: Of course you can communicate with me directly.

Q: Don't take offence. . . .

HEYM: No, no. Excuse me if I sounded offended or if I sounded a little bit amazed. I'll give you my address and my phone number. If you write a letter, you must figure that it takes about two weeks for it to reach me because it's being read.

At the request of the publishers Stefan Heym wrote the following statement to supplement the information contained in the preceding interview.

On April 10, 1973, *Neues Deutschland*, official organ of the Socialist Unity Party, carried a two-column story on Stefan Heym in which the paper's editors sprinkled him with faint praise as *an author firmly allied with us in the struggle against imperialism.* The item closed with the surprise announcement:

> Stefan Heym's new historical novel, *The King David Report,* is being prepared for publication in the GDR.

Neues Deutschland proved to be well informed: in the weeks following, Heym signed contracts with East German publishers not only for *The King David Report* but also for his novel on Lassalle, *Uncertain Friend*, and for his *Queen Against Defoe*, the three titles previously taboo in the German Democratic Republic.

Journalists and others have queried Heym as to the reasons for the sudden turnabout. There was no certain answer, Heym told them, but there was the story of a conversation he had with a comrade then quite powerful in the field of arts and letters. This comrade stated he might consider publishing the Lassalle book, after some changes of course, but *Defoe*—never!

Heym recalls having replied, "I'm afraid this is a question of identification. If you identify yourself with the Earl of Nottingham, then you can't possibly permit this book to be printed in the GDR, just as Nottingham could only try to suppress Defoe's *The Shortest Way with the Dissenters* in the England of Queen Anne. But if your heart is with Defoe the revolutionary, as the heart of a Communist should be, then it is your damned duty to have the book published here."

The logic of the argument apparently prevailed; the GDR authorities gave in to their Communist conscience.